MW00329093

THE TREACHERY
OF
RUSSIAN NESTING DOLLS

ALSO BY OREST STELMACH

The Boy from Reactor 4

The Boy Who Stole from the Dead

The Boy Who Glowed in the Dark

The Altar Girl

THE

TREACHERY

OF

RUSSIAN

NESTING DOLLS

This is a work of fiction. Names, characters, organizations, places, events, and incidents are either products of the author's imagination or are used fictitiously.

Copyright 2017 © Orest Stelmach
All rights reserved.

No part of this book may be reproduced, or stored in a retrieval system, or transmitted in any form or by any means, electronic, mechanical, photocopying, recording, or otherwise, without express written permission of the author.

www.oreststelmach.com

ISBN-13: 9780692995280
ISBN-10: 0692995285

Cover design by David Drummond

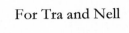
For Tra and Nell

CHAPTER 1

The best way to find someone who doesn't want to be found is to make him search for you.

For an American woman in a foreign country, that can be problematic. Fortunately, I was in Amsterdam. Most people come to Amsterdam in search of something. You can find anything you want and all of it is legal. All I had to do to find the murder victim's secret lover was to become what he wanted.

It took me four days to make the necessary arrangements. The biggest impediment to my mission was my American passport. The landlords who rented the type of office I needed leased space only to tenants with EU passports. I finally found one who was willing to make an exception in the spirit of international cooperation. My offer to pay a fifty percent premium in rent may have played a small role, too.

The landlady's office was located on a canal with Venetian views and a pair of majestic white swans near a bar called the Black Tiger in the city's oldest section. The landlady greeted me at the door with a chilling once-over that left me fearing I'd gone too far this time. She looked like a sewer-dwelling cannibal who'd snuck above ground to lure her next meal to her nest, latex skin stretched taut over a bare skeleton disguised by a designer suit. If her profit were threatened, I could picture her crossing the threshold from stark to stark raving mad and consuming my body. God only knew what she'd suffered to become the woman she appeared to be today.

I sat across from her at a barebones metal desk, gave her my passport, and answered questions about my background. Her English accent sounded Moroccan or Algerian, not Dutch. That made sense because she was probably connected to organized crime. A Netherlands crime organization was less like a Sicilian family and more like a social media network, a collection of nodes that called upon each other to help with the drug and sex trade throughout Europe. That didn't make it any less dangerous when crossed.

After the landlady finished her questionnaire, she asked me to fill out some paperwork. Some parts were for her employers, others for the city of Amsterdam. Then she studied her notes like a teacher grading a test. When she was finished she perused them again, as though she couldn't fail me but was looking for a reason to do so.

"Your application is in order," she finally said, with a note of reluctance. "But I must ask you once more. Are you certain you want to do this?"

"I'm certain," I said.

"You understand why I'm asking. We don't get many women … many women like you."

"Like me?"

She looked me over again to make her point.

I knew what she meant. I was educated, American, and over thirty.

"Yes. Women who answer questions with a question," she said. "Women like you."

"I told you. It's a fantasy of mine. It's on my bucket list."

"Bucket list?"

"A list of things a person wants to do before she dies," I said.

The landlady shook her head as though that made no sense. "You understand that the owners of this business are very serious men. If you are planning on conducting any illegal business from your office, they will deal with you quickly and severely."

Her words jolted me. The warning didn't surprise me, but the landlady's blunt delivery hit me hard. Once again I wondered if I was being too brazen for my own good.

"I won't be using the room to conduct any business other than the one for which it's intended," I said.

The landlord appraised me one more time. Her pen hovered over the signature page as though her instincts were warning her that I might have an ulterior motive. If those were, in fact, her instincts, they were spot-on.

"Seventy-five euro a night for ten nights," she said.

"Agreed."

"You pay every day by four o'clock."

"No. I'm going to pay you in full right now. For all ten days."

The landlord lifted her eyebrows a smidge. It was the first time I noticed she had any.

I pulled seven hundred and fifty euro from my wallet and placed them on her desk. She collected the money, signed the lease and gave me a copy.

I savored a rush of adrenaline. There was no turning back now. I was committed to my mission. And yet the walls closed in on me a bit, too. The process of renting an office had been very professional. I was here of my own volition and I'd been treated respectfully, by a woman, no less. Still, I detected an undercurrent of exploitation. It was as though a syringe had tapped my soul when I'd signed on the dotted line.

We walked across the canal and continued two blocks further to a parallel street. The *Oude Kerk*, the medieval city's original stone church, stood in the center of a square. My new office was located on the periphery of the quaint, circular walkway surrounding the church. It faced the Puccini Bomboni chocolate shop at the base of the church's towering steeple, and a small café with outdoor seating. I was dying to try a sea salt caramel truffle from Puccini but duty prevented me from consuming any chocolate for now. Duty was, indeed, a bitch. I glanced at my feet on and off as we circled around the church. The cobblestones along *Oudekerksplein* were notoriously uneven.

My office was located on the ground floor of an antique brick apartment building. We entered via a back door, passed a room with a vintage washer and dryer, and a dingy bathroom, and arrived at my new work place. It consisted of one room. A single bed occupied one corner. A high chair faced a floor-to-ceiling window. Its shade was pulled down. There was a second door beside the window. It opened onto the street.

The landlady pointed to a circular button attached to the wall.

"Panic button," she said.

"Who's going to come to my rescue?" I said.

"The Turk will come."

"What does he look like?"

The landlady pressed the button.

I glanced at my watch to measure the response time. Twenty seconds later a man came thundering down the hallway into my office. He arrived with muscles bunched and eyes bent on rectifying a wrong. He resembled a pallet-flinging, bone-breaking longshoreman who had rendered cranes and robots unnecessary in his day. His face was the size of a dinner plate and as handsome as the pan in which the roast had burnt. He had to stoop to get into the room, and as soon as he opened his mouth to speak, the blast of garlic almost knocked me out.

He spoke in Dutch and the landlady answered him accordingly. He relaxed once he heard what she had to say, and gave me his version of the once-over.

"American?" he said.

The landlady had seen my passport. I couldn't lie even though I wanted to for some reason, as though being an American put me at greater risk outside the borders of my home country. This, in turn, pissed me off.

"That's right," I said. "I'm an American."

He nodded with an unsettling mixture of determination and glee. "Good," he said, in decent English. "I'm going to be your first customer." With that seemingly business-like proclamation, he turned and disappeared.

The mere prospect of his intentions trumped most of the trials and tribulations of my life and rendered them cake-eating celebrations. I had become too clever for my own good. In fact, I was insane. A sinking feeling gripped me.

The landlady handed me the key. "Good luck," she said.

I took the key and thanked her. She exited via the rear door also. By the time she was gone I'd calmed myself down the way I always did, by reminding myself there was always a way out of any situation, and that the woman who controlled her emotions would eventually find it.

I returned to my hotel. I worked out at the gym, tanned in the solarium, and ate two egg whites with a side of spinach, which would be my only meal of the day. I'd deprived myself of carbohydrates for the last four days and had rinsed most of the water out from under my skin. At nine o'clock I packed my tote bag and marched back to my new office. I'd decided to open up at ten o'clock, two hours before their ritual meeting. If the mystery lover didn't come at midnight, I'd stay open until two in the morning. I'd allow a four-hour window just in case this was the one time that circumstances made him early or late.

I walked to work dreaming of unlimited carbohydrate consumption. But this gnawing yearning for relief was accompanied by a sense of exultation. For the first time in my life I didn't loathe or dislike my naked body. My nutritional deprivation had also left me with an eerie high. This hyper-awareness kept me nimble and helped me avoid the onslaught of bicyclists along the roads. It was a steady flow of gorgeous and fit people of all ages speeding to their destinations in pursuit of constant fulfillment, and seemingly indifferent to any pedestrian casualties that might ensue. I loathed the perpetual impediment they posed while fantasizing about their quality of life.

When I arrived at my office, I went into the bathroom and began to transform myself. I slipped into a caramel-colored wig with a ponytail. Then I put on a fluorescent green bikini, strapped on a pair of matching three-inch pumps, and wrapped a pair of lime-colored Revo sunglasses around my head. When I was done, I looked like the product of a deviant affair between an independent urban woman and a praying mantis.

I opened a half liter bottle of still water and put it on the high chair beside me. The prior tenant had liked to stay hydrated. Then I affixed my MP3 player onto a portable dock with two small speakers and placed it beside the water. The prior tenant also had been a heavy metal girl who liked the eighties even though she hadn't been born until the nineties. Her favorite group was a German rock band called the Scorpions, and she listened to their greatest hits in a continuous loop while she worked.

I pressed play. A guitar screamed, drums pounded. One of my brother's favorite rock anthems started up.

My transformation was complete. I now resembled the prior tenant, the girl whose murder I'd been hired to investigate. According to my client, the dead girl was a bit narrower in the shoulders and hips, but one had to be looking to really notice it. All I wanted was for her lover to knock on the door at midnight the way he always did on Saturdays. All I needed was to see him face-to-face and ask him some questions. There was a risk he knew she was dead and wouldn't come, but my client doubted it. They'd only met at her office and only on Saturday nights. The eccentricity of their meetings had fueled their passion for the last two months. According to my client, they were falling in love when the girl was killed.

I was more than a bit apprehensive as I approached the floor-to-ceiling window. I imagined yanking the curtain aside and making myself visible. Initially I would feel hopelessly conspicuous. That much was certain, but I had experienced enough adversity in life to know that I would quickly get used to my new circumstances. I wondered if I would feel empowered or humiliated and the effect on my self-esteem if no buyers knocked on my door. It would crush my fragile female ego. The only thing worse would be a steady flow of customers.

I shrugged my insecurity aside. My concerns were to be expected. They were also irrelevant. The only thing that mattered was the job. The mystery lover was out there. Tonight he would come looking for his girl. I had become his girl. Hence, tonight he would come looking for me.

The song's refrain poured from the speakers:

Here I am, rock you like a hurricane.

I felt as ridiculous as the lyrics sounded. But looking and sounding authentic were prerequisites to completing the assignment I'd accepted. Contrary to the popular saying, failure was an option – it was always an option. But if I failed to complete this assignment, I'd be deeply disappointed because I was working for my most important client. So I pushed aside my self-consciousness, took a final deep breath, exhaled, and pulled the curtain open.

Dark shadows enveloped the *Oude Kerk*. The oldest section of Amsterdam, named *De Wallen* after the retaining walls that once stood here, was also Amsterdam's best known red-light district. Tourists were still ambling by, but the chocolate shop had closed, a pair of creepy men with turned-up collars sat drinking beer out-

14

side the café, and a rowdy group of Englishmen was approaching. I sensed a passive form of aggression in the air, though admittedly, I was wearing sunglasses and everything seemed dark to me. I walked over to the second door, the one that would open my office to the men trolling *De Wallen* tonight, and flicked a switch on the wall. Two incandescent red lights came alive above the exterior of my window. I stood five feet back from the window, the prior tenant's preferred position, and sipped from the giant water bottle.

Here I am, rock you like a hurricane.

I was now legally employed as a sex worker in Amsterdam. I was a window prostitute. I was as far from the Ukrainian Catholic altar girl I'd been as a child as a woman could get.

Nadia Tesla was open for business.

CHAPTER 2

Window prostitutes disliked being gawked at by tourists because they interfered with the seduction of the self-conscious but real buyer. Personally, I didn't mind the tourists. Nor did I mind the solitary Asian, Nigerian, or German-looking men walking back and forth along the same street as though they were on their way to the Anne Frank museum but got lost. What unnerved me were the occasional gangs of burly men who looked mean and angry. They didn't smile, laugh, or appear to be having fun of any kind. Hate, not lust, shone in their eyes. They didn't look like men who wanted me. They looked like men who wanted to kill me.

And as that thought flitted through my mind, someone cast a shadow against my window and I heard a knock on my door. To the other women in my newfound trade, it would have been the sound of opportunity. But to me it was the sound of reckoning, for even without seeing his face, I knew who'd come a-calling.

My pulse pounded. I took a breath and cracked the door open.

But where I expected to see the Turk's nausea-inducing face, I saw nothing but air. In fact, I had to look down to waist-level to see my first customer. A man in his mid-twenties with tousled brown hair sat overflowing a wheelchair. He gazed at me with a heart-wrenching innocence made all the more earnest by the round spectacles that made his eyes look like saucers.

He cracked his lips to speak but couldn't manage any words. He gave a little croak instead, as though either my physique or ensemble had taken his breath away. I preferred to think it was the former though I wasn't one to discriminate between compliments.

I searched for something to say myself but did no better. In fact, a bolt of anxiety wracked me. I hadn't contemplated a scenario where a sympathetic-looking man tried to engage my services. I hadn't considered the prospect of feeling a little bit guilty for saying no. Yet here I was, standing in front of a young man who probably couldn't get sex any other way. And out of four hundred or so window prostitutes in Amsterdam, he'd chosen me.

Another unexpected emotion hit me. Not only had I experienced a stab of guilt, I was a bit flush from flattery.

We both stood there looking at each other until he finally took his eyes off the ripples in my abdomen and looked beyond me into my dimly lit office. His head began bobbing up and down slightly, and I was reminded that there was music playing in the background.

"Scorpions," he said, with a lovely English accent. "That's very nice." His eyes drifted to my torso before he pulled them back up. "There's no one like you."

If I hadn't been tanned, he might have seen me blush. "That's very sweet of you ..."

"No. I mean the Scorpions song. *There's No One Like You.* That's my favorite – wait, you're American?" He frowned as though this was a shocking observation, which of course, I was sure it was.

"I'm a citizen of the world," I said.

"Don't think I saw any American women on my last trip. Can I come in and listen to the Scorpions with you?"

"I'm sorry, honey," I said. "I don't think that's realistic."

"Just kidding. I had something in mind along your usual line of business. How much for half an hour? I know the standard time is fifteen minutes, but it takes me a little longer ... "

"I'm sorry, really I am ..."

"No, no. My John Thomas works. You don't have to worry about that. All I want is a little rumpy-pumpy. Nothing kinky. Just a little ride on my motorbike will do. Look ..." He fumbled with a fanny pack. "I'm minted. I can show you."

I bent down, put my hand on his, and gave it a sympathetic squeeze. "You need to find another girl."

"Oh. I understand."

His eyes turned to slits. He maneuvered a lever. The motor attached to his wheelchair whirred. The wheels rolled backward.

"No," I said. "It's not that. This has nothing to do with your handicap."

He stopped the wheelchair mid-turn and glanced at me one last time. "Then what does it have to do with?"

I couldn't be honest with him and to lie would have been an even bigger insult. I shook my head. "I'm sorry. I can't explain."

The young man in the wheelchair considered my words and nodded. "Yeah. I like that one, too."

I had no idea what he was talking about. "Excuse me?"

He measured me head-to-toe once more, this time with a look of disgust appropriate for a fraud. "*I Can't Explain*. It's a song. Do you even like the Scorpions?" He shook his head. "Bloody Yanks. Can't trust them. Can't shag them, either." He wheeled himself away.

I closed the door and headed straight for the water, wishing it were wine instead. Every *De Wallen* window girl has the legal right to quote any price for any service and to turn away any potential customer for no reason whatsoever. That's what gave me the audacity to set up shop in the first place. I figured I needed to open my door and appear to be congenial, lest someone start rapping on my window and create a scene. But I didn't need to even quote a price to anyone for any kind of service if I didn't want to. And I sure as hell didn't want to.

I thought posing as a window prostitute would be deceptively straightforward, but like most enterprises that came with such expectations, it was obviously going to be the opposite.

I returned to my post five feet from the window, smiling and flashing my teeth to the occasional solitary passer-by, swaying my hips a barely perceptible amount to the beat, trying not to look as preposterous as I felt.

If only the faithful from my childhood church could have seen me now. I pictured them gasping collectively and covering their mouths with shock and dismay. I imagined my mother shaking her head, criticizing my figure, the clothes, and the wig. The thought of my deceased father seeing me caused my face to burn. There were no circumstances under which he would have accepted my standing in this window. He would have told me I was too intelligent and educated for such a masquerade. He would have expected me to be making a living in a more elegant fashion. In fact, all enterprises that promote elegance have roots in the gutter.

The same could have been said about my dead husband, who'd been a professor of religion at Yale. He would have called me trash and dashed off into the arms of his adoring graduate assistant. Given that assessment, you'd think my ex-husband was the one who mattered to me the least. But life is not that logical. It was, in fact, he who mattered the most. It was the image of his car wrapped around an oak tree a mile from my mother's house and his subsequent funeral that still persecuted me.

The next hour and forty-five minutes went by slowly. The only action came courtesy of a Spanish-looking man in his sixties. He pretended to be taking pictures of his wife but he'd positioned her so that he could zoom in on the three African girls in the windows around the bend from me.

Taking pictures of the working girls in *De Wallen* is a no-no. The Turk appeared out of nowhere, barked something at him, ripped the camera from his hands and confiscated its memory card. Then he disappeared. The tourist and his wife looked around for help, but even if they'd found the police, they would have gotten little sympathy from the law on this matter.

At first, the sight of the Turk unsettled me, his earlier promise to be my first customer still fresh in my mind. But then I took comfort in knowing that someone was manning the panic button and that he obviously took his responsibility seriously.

I thought I was going to get to midnight without having to open the door again, but at eleven-thirty my neighborhood began to bustle with drunken activity. A group of six Welshmen on a stag party wanted the prospective groom to enjoy a final fling with the "mullato devil woman." I guessed the combination of my tan, the dim lighting, and their drunken state had turned me into an exotic creature, and I was quite flattered by the description. They were less flattered when I turned them away on account of my alleged allergy to alcohol. One of them questioned my choice of occupation, but by then the others had spied the African girls around the bend and they continued onward without major incident.

I turned away two more drunken men in their thirties who spoke French, and a polite Japanese salary man in his fifties. None of them gave me any trouble. I had one eye on my watch at 11:55 and butterflies were swirling in my stomach when someone knocked on the door yet again. I stepped closer to the window and glanced to my left.

It was the Turk. He motioned for me to open-up.

I considered ignoring him but I knew that wouldn't work. He would step in front of my window and demand that I open the door. If he became persistent, he might scare away the mystery lover.

A fist pounded on the door. I heard something that sounded like English but I couldn't make out the words.

I hit the panic button three times rapidly, took a deep breath, and ran to the door. I whipped it open and stood nose-to-chest with the Turk.

"Where the hell have you been?" I said.

A slight grin crossed his lips. "You've been wanting me from the moment you saw me—"

"Not exactly—"

"Relax. The Turk is going to give you satisfaction."

"I hit the panic button three times. Three times. And where were you?"

He'd started to push past me but my words made him freeze. "Panic button? When?"

"Just now, a minute ago, constantly. What does it matter? Where were you? Is anyone looking out for me? Anyone at all?"

"I have a colleague—"

"Who's obviously incompetent."

The Turk blinked twice and looked me over again, this time with concern. "What happened?"

"A man tried to force himself on me. We agreed on a price and took care of some business, but then he wanted something extra. When I refused, he stole his money back and said if I tried to do anything about it he'd follow me home after work some day and beat me."

"He said this?"

"How can you expect me to take care of you if you don't take care of me? Is this the Dutch way? Is this the Turkish way?"

"I am not Turkish," he said slowly, as though simultaneously thinking about the matter at hand. "I'm Greek."

I heard a ruckus behind me and then the sound of footsteps clattering toward my office. A man arrived in a huff from the inside of the building. He looked like the Turk's younger cousin. He said something in Dutch that included the words "panic button" in English. The Turk replied sharply, his protégé gave him some lip in return, and the Turk barked what sounded like a final order at him. The younger bodyguard lowered his head and disappeared from my office the same way he'd arrived.

I checked my watch. It was midnight. The mystery lover might be arriving any second.

"What did this man look like?" the Turk said.

"He was in his mid-twenties. Tall, thin, blonde hair and blue eyes. He was American. Can you believe that? From Los Angeles."

"Really." The Turk sounded as though I'd just whetted his appetite for combat. "Did you see which way he went?"

"To the right. When he first came in he said he was making a pit stop before going to the Bulldog Café."

"Cannabis," the Turk said with disgust. "But there are several Bulldog Cafes."

"Then why are you still here?"

The Turk muttered something under his breath, started to leave, and then turned back and devoured me with a final look. "Don't close before you see me tonight." His words sounded way too much like an order for my liking, but he took off before I could say anything.

Just as the Turk vanished out of sight, a young man stopped near my door. His eyes met mine. I knew right away this was my mark. I knew it because he was wearing a hoodie. No one in Amsterdam wore a hoodie. It was a silly disguise, the kind that made one stand out even more. I also knew he was the one because he was so gorgeous. Raised cheekbones, skin so smooth a woman might be afraid to touch it, and aquamarine eyes that mesmerized and weakened the knees.

A sinking feeling washed over me. I'd blown it. If I'd been in the office, standing five feet back from the window in the semi-darkness, he wouldn't have seen me clearly. He wouldn't have realized I wasn't his girl until he came inside and saw me in person. But I wasn't in my office, I was in the doorway three feet away from him.

His eyes widened, his lips parted. He took a step back—

"Wait," I said.

But he didn't wait.

He turned and hurried away.

CHAPTER 3

I took off my high-heels and sunglasses and tossed them onto the chair. I grabbed the sweatshirt I'd brought, zipped it up to my neck, and slipped into my flat shoes. Then I slammed the door shut and took off after the mystery lover. All I needed was ten seconds of face-time to explain to him that I was his friend, not his enemy. That I wanted to solve the murder of his beloved, not cause him any additional despair.

I had no time to change into pants. I knew I was about to make a spectacle of myself and I didn't relish the prospect. I cherished stealth and anonymity. I loathed the thought of drawing attention to myself in any way, especially given I was a guest in a foreign country. My suitcase didn't contain blue jeans when I travelled abroad. Europe was a classier place than America and I packed accordingly. Now, here I was hustling across the *Oudekerkplein* in a bikini bottom. I didn't resemble the prototypical American tourist in shorts and tank top. I made that get-up look civilized.

And yet I didn't hesitate. The pin-prick of embarrassment was just that. I'd snuck my cousin out of Chornobyl and into New York via Siberia. I'd stared down the cops on the Trans Siberian

Railway by posing as a journalist, cajoled a cemetery caretaker to unearth a grave in Ukraine, and convinced a billionaire to fly me around the world by pretending to not want his help. A woman's will could propel her to act outside of social norms to achieve her goals. The prerequisite to harnessing that will was the willingness to risk failure.

My flats had thin soles. As a result, the cobblestones threw off my balance. I had trouble walking a straight line. I suspected I looked drunk. A few jaws dropped. Some pedestrians moved to the side to make way for me. Men loitering near bars craned their necks for a better view. I ignored them.

The secret lover marched purposefully but didn't run. He didn't want to attract attention to himself, I thought. Smart boy. All eyes were focused on me instead of him. I was determined to catch-up to him with a walking pace honed on New York City sidewalks. Running would only make me stand out even more. I'd rarely failed to catch up to anyone along Madison Avenue. I didn't see any reason I wouldn't do so now.

"Wait," I said. "I'm a friend. I want to help you. I want to help Iskra."

Iskra was the name of the deceased girl. I shouted at her mystery lover from behind but he either didn't hear me or wasn't interested in what I had to say. He simply kept walking like a robot programmed to stay ahead of me.

I followed him right onto *Warmoesstraat*, still twenty paces back. I passed a corner store specializing in whips and chains, and an illuminated houseboat on the canal where two couples were enjoying dinner. A bicycle wrapped in white lights sparkled in the picture window of a luxury row house beyond them.

We'd walked a city block and I'd gained no ground at all. The mystery lover had long legs and could move. Damned if he didn't have longer legs and wasn't fitter than I was. In half a block he would reach the outer border of De Wallen. There was simply no way I could leave *De Wallen* in my current state of dress.

I began to jog. My feet stung and I wished I were wearing trainers. I repeated my plea for him to stop and that I was his friend.

He didn't respond. He reached the border of *De Wallen*, turned right onto a side street, and disappeared.

I ran.

When I reached the corner I saw him climbing into the back of a small SUV. I didn't recognize the vehicle. From my viewpoint, I could see a short vertical post in the middle of the road directly in front of the vehicle's bumper with a vivid red light. I could also see that the mystery lover was seated in the back of the SUV, but only the driver was seated in front. The front passenger seat was empty. The SUV's break lights shone red. Any second the driver would switch into reverse and come barreling toward me, I thought.

I hugged the buildings along the right sidewalk and raced toward the vehicle. I was ten strides away. Five strides . . . I read the lettering on the back of the SUV. It was a Porsche Macan Turbo . . . Three strides away . . . I caught a glimpse of the license plate—

The brake lights dimmed. The engine whirred. The sound of God's vacuum cleaner filled the air. The SUV surged forward, turned left, and disappeared.

I took my final three strides and stood over the cap of the small vertical post. It had sunken into the ground. Its light was green now.

My chest heaved as I swore to myself. A light sheen of sweat covered my forehead. I felt completely naked and embarrassed. I turned and began to jog back toward *Warmoesstraat*. I was technically half a block beyond *De Wallen*. I hoped one of the residents along the canal or in the houseboat hadn't seen me and been offended.

A siren wailed. It was a European police siren, a long squeeze of the horn followed by a short one. It was more measured than the frenetic American version. Under other circumstances, I might have enjoyed the sound and the moment. But these weren't other circumstances.

A white hatchback with diagonal blue and red stripes across the doorway pulled up to the corner in front of me. I'd never imagined my undoing in Amsterdam would come via a vehicle painted red, white and blue. Two cops dressed in fluorescent yellow vests and white uniforms stepped out of the car. A third cop pulled up on a bicycle. He wore a sidearm like the other two and a puffed-up olive bomber jacket that looked like a Gore-Tex model designed for Arctic discothèques.

They asked me for identification. I told them I didn't have any. They asked me who I was. I stuck to my two stories, that I was an American woman living out a fantasy and that one of my customers had robbed me. From that point on they regarded me with a mixture of suspicion and compassion. They didn't laugh at me. They didn't appear to judge me. I imagined a similar situation in New York City and how some of the cops might have treated me there, and felt a sudden love for the people of the Netherlands and all things Dutch. Even the bicyclists.

The feel-good didn't last long. They took my description of the phantom blond American who'd robbed me. I swallowed my guilt as I delivered my fictitious story. The cop on the bicycle took notes. Then all three of them drove me back to my office. They let me change into my business suit and told me to gather my things. While one of the cops stayed with me, the other two canvassed the neighborhood. They spoke with seemingly random onlookers. Then the Turk materialized, out of nowhere as usual, and they spoke with him. I assumed he was verifying I had a lease and confirming my story that I'd been robbed and had hit the panic button.

Before they returned to my office, I thought the cops would scold me and let me go. But once they arrived I could see that their interviews had drained them of their compassion for me. One of them pulled out a high-tech-looking, hinged pair of handcuffs. I looked at them with dread.

"You're arresting me?" I said. Dejection punctuated my voice.

"You were heard shouting at the young man," the cop said, "trying to solicit him on the street. That's against the law. Prostitution is legal but only in certain places."

"I wasn't trying to solicit him——"

"You were heard shouting at him. That you wanted to 'help him.' Why would you want to help him if he robbed you?"

I realized his point.

"And your protection said that one of his colleagues told him that no such man ever entered your room. He said no one entered your room tonight. No one at all. Did you know they watch the doorways through binoculars from across the street?"

My lies had caught up with me.

I searched frantically for solace of some kind, and found it in my memory banks. I'd seen the getaway car and committed the license plate to memory. Still, when the police officer shackled me with his handcuffs I suppressed a tear. I was surprised at the depth of my emotions, but I'd never been arrested before and until it happens to you it's impossible to understand the loss of self-respect. For the moment, a highly civilized country had decided its society was better off if I was denied freedom to do as I pleased. It was, much to my shock, a remarkably depressing moment.

Yet it was not nearly as devastating as the scene that transpired when I climbed into the back of the police car. I was trying not to look embarrassed but also avoiding the eyes of the bystanders who'd gathered along the street. Curiosity got the better of me, though, and when I glanced at the crowd of thirty or so, I spotted the last person I wanted to see. I averted my eyes from his, an exercise in pathetic wishful thinking, and then looked back. No, I was not seeing a mirage. He was here. My client was here.

Simeon Simeonovich stood twenty yards away looking like a modern-day Cossack without the horse, handsome and stoic in a turtleneck and one of the half-zip Italian sweaters he favored. Brunello Cucinelli, I guessed. I recognized one of his bodyguards beside him, but didn't see the second one. That was strange because he was always accompanied by a pair.

Our eyes met for a brief moment. I gave Simmy as neutral a stare as I could muster, determined not to reveal anything about my state of mind. More than anything, though, I was secretly praying to see a flicker of compassion in his eyes. But I saw only the steely gaze of a Russian oligarch, the thirty-seventh richest man in the world. And beneath that gaze I spied disappointment and disapproval.

What the hell was he doing here?

When the policeman closed the door beside me, it shut with audible finality. It drowned out all the noise from the street and left me alone, sunken in cheap leather and despair. I was not the most ingenious and resourceful woman in the world. I was the stupid American woman on her way to jail for prostitution in a city where prostitution was legal.

I really had gone too far this time.

The police car pulled away from *Oudekerksplein*.

Nadia Tesla was closed for business.

CHAPTER 4

My visit to the Amsterdam police station didn't go exactly as I expected. I should have been prepared to be treated like a criminal but I was distracted by my plight. Not only had I been arrested, Simmy had seen it happen. That meant I had to extricate myself from criminal prosecution and salvage my relationship with my most important client. Multi-tasking life-altering emergencies can obscure one's focus.

That focus sharpened as soon as they put me in a room with eight cops. They entered without their firearms. One of them, the only one under six-feet tall, stood apart from the others, looking at me as though I were Interpol's Most Wanted. He whispered orders. The room buzzed at his command. The duo who'd arrested me removed my belt and confiscated my shoe laces. Another cop took inventory of all the things in my tote bag and had me sign it. They all spoke impeccable English and the entire exercise echoed with military precision.

I knew better than to complain or ask for preferential treatment. I did, however, inquire if I was entitled to a phone call and a lawyer. The cops who arrested me told me I had to be processed first. When they were done, a fresh-faced rookie escorted me to a jail cell and locked me inside. The jail cell looked like Mr. Clean's training room. It contained a cot, a stainless steel sink, and a toilet. A camera hung in a corner where the walls met the ceiling.

I alternated sitting on my cot and pacing the jail cell, wondering how much damage I'd done to my reputation and my relationship with Simmy. An hour later, a man in a sports jacket and tie arrived with a clipboard and my passport. He introduced himself as Detective De Vroom. He had olive skin, lush brown hair parted to the side, and full lips. But it was the condescending look in his eyes that revealed his character to me. He was one of those men who believed that the handsomest and most talented man on Earth could be seen in his mirror every time he looked in it.

He asked me my name and address even though he had my passport. After I answered him, he moved on to more provocative questions.

"Do you know of any of crimes involving drugs that are about to take place?" he said.

"No."

"Do you know of any crimes involving the trafficking of women for the purpose of sexual exploitation that are about to take place?"

I told him I didn't.

"Do you know any women working as prostitutes in Amsterdam below the age of twenty-one?"

The minimum legal age for Amsterdam prostitutes was twenty-one.

"I don't know any other prostitutes in Amsterdam, let alone minors," I said.

I realized I'd just called myself a prostitute. *That wasn't true. I was just pretending, and yet I was the one who'd rented the window, right?*

His eyes bored into mine. "You're in serious trouble, Ms. Tesla."

A sinking sensation hit me. "What do you mean?"

"The Dutch legal system used to be the most liberal in Europe. Unfortunately for you, it's now become the most severe. The Netherlands is a hub for transit crime. Women are routinely smuggled from Eastern Europe and Africa through our borders to the rest of the EU. Illegal prostitution usually involves minors or immigrants being forced to work against their will. That's why illegal prostitution is a very serious crime here, even if the offense is street-walking."

"But I'm not forcing a minor or any woman to do anything against her will. And I wasn't really street-walking. You know that, Detective. Please. I pay rent for a room with a window. Why the hell would I be street-walking?"

"Any kind of behavior that remotely appears to be illegal prostitution is dealt with severely in Holland. You may not get jail time, or even go to court. But you'll have to hire an attorney to negotiate a transaction with the prosecutor's office. That's similar to what you Americans call a plea bargain. The American consulate will have to be notified. At a minimum, you'll be deported and labeled an undesirable by member countries of the European Union. You'll never be allowed in Europe again."

"That's ridiculous," I said.

He shrugged. "You Americans are experts in the ridiculous."

A powerful government and its police could make almost anything happen to any person. I imagined never being allowed to enter Europe again. I had a sudden urge to vomit, find a time capsule, or jump into one of Amsterdam's finest canals, preferably drunk.

But then a calm descended upon me. De Vroom had entered my cell channeling hostility. His interview had consisted of a series of escalating threats. On the surface, his goal was to scare me, one which he'd accomplished. The question was, what did he really want from me?

"Your warning about what might happen to me is duly noted, Detective," I said. "But I sense you have something else in mind."

He frowned. "I beg your pardon?"

"I'll be deported and labeled an undesirable throughout the EU for a trumped-up charge of illegal prostitution – let's be serious, all I did was run through the streets in a bikini bottom – unless I do something. Something for the Netherlands, something for the Amsterdam police, or more likely, something to further your career, Detective De Vroom. So tell me, what do I know that you want to know?"

De Vroom eyes narrowed a smidge, just enough to tell me I'd surprised him. "Why did you lie to the officers who arrested you?"

"Who said I lied?"

"You said the man you were chasing robbed you, but your own protection said no man ever entered your room. And what was it a witness heard you say?" De Vroom flipped to a page attached to his clipboard. "'I'm your friend. I want to help you. I want to help Iskra.' Who is Iskra?"

"Not who, what," I said. "*Iskra* means 'spark.' Your witnesses must have been hearing things. Aren't a variety of recreational drugs sold in the coffee shops and nutritional stores along the streets of *De Wallen*? Can you really trust any of those witnesses?"

"Why did you rent a room and pretend to be a window prostitute?"

"Pretend? I paid the rent. I wore a bikini, high heels, stood in a floor-to-ceiling window and interacted with customers."

"Iskra is the name of the prostitute who rented the same room you worked. She was murdered a week ago."

"Murdered?" I said.

"Yes. Murdered. You know her name. You know where she worked. You know she was murdered. That I understand. What I don't understand is why a forensic financial analyst from America is investigating her murder. That is what you are doing, because if you'd been hired for some sort of financial investigation, you wouldn't be chasing after young men in *De Wallen* shouting the dead girl's name, would you?"

I shrugged.

"Why are you here, in Amsterdam?" he said.

"To see the canals, eat some of your fine Indonesian food, and find out why a girl was killed."

"That's my job. I don't need help from tourists."

"Really? Who's lying now?" I waited a beat. "Let me remind you of some recent history. Malaysia Airlines flight number seventeen headed from Amsterdam to Kuala Lumpur crashed in the Donetsk Oblast of Ukraine on July 17, 2014. Of the two hundred and eighty-three passengers, two-thirds were citizens of the Netherlands. The overwhelming evidence is that so-called pro-Russian separatists shot the plane down accidentally. But the advanced weapons system they used to destroy the plane was supplied by the Russian government and the so-called separatists were actually thugs on the Russian payroll. The reaction in Holland against Russians was swift and severe. Russians became personae non gratae. Many fled the country back to their homeland. Those that didn't keep a low profile. The downside for you is that the Russians who stayed have no love loss for the Dutch authorities, who did not exactly shed tears for their sudden persecution, in the press and on the sidewalks. You need me because Iskra Romanova was Russian and no Russian is going to cooperate with you."

"But they'll cooperate with you? An American? Why is that?"

"Because I'm fluent in the language and I bring impeccable references."

"Whose references?"

I didn't answer.

"Impress me with what you know so far."

"Iskra was attached to a wall in the form of a crucifix. The killer cut the feminine parts from the rest of her body. She died by bleeding out. You thought it might have been the result of a botched burglary by the notorious Van Hassell gang – they have super violent tendencies – but now you're not sure it was a burglary at all. Cash, jewelry and a painting were stolen. But another stash of cash and some antique silverware weren't taken."

De Vroom considered what I'd said for a moment. "You're working for the family."

"I can't and won't comment on my client's identity. That is non-negotiable no matter what the implications are for me."

He raised his chin in a manner that seemed like a compliment to me, as though I'd finally done something to impress him.

"Tell me about this man you lured to your room by dressing like Iskra," he said. "This man you followed and lost."

"What will the spirit of cooperation earn me?"

"You haven't been formally charged with any crime yet. We could pretend this entire business never happened. And no one would ever be the wiser that you were ever in this jail."

"Not enough."

"Not enough? You must be joking. What else do you want?"

"A partnership. I'll tell you what I know about the man I tried to lure to my nest. Iskra's nest, I should say. Then I'll give you the license plate of the car he jumped into right before your colleagues arrested me."

"And in exchange?"

"You give me the name of the owner of the car after you run the plates. Then I stay in Amsterdam and keep working the case from inside the community. We share any valuable information, the kind that can lead to the murderer's arrest – beneficial to you – and keep me from harm's way – beneficial to me."

"That is not realistic," De Vroom said.

"But this is Amsterdam. Things that are not realistic in other cities are entirely possible here."

"We don't consult with civilians on police matters."

"You're not consulting with me," I said. "I'm consulting with you out of respect and self-interest."

De Vroom thought about what I'd said. "Tell me about Iskra's mystery lover."

I told him what I knew.

"You have no idea who he is?" De Vroom said.

"No."

"And no one in the Russian community knows either?"

"I don't know the community well enough to go that far," I said. "I doubt he's a suspect. He wouldn't have come to her room tonight if he knew she were dead, if he'd killed her himself."

"You have a lot to learn. Everyone is a suspect until the perpetrator is found. You'd be surprised how often criminals return to the scene of their crimes."

De Vroom asked me some more questions, mostly going over the facts I'd just revealed. When we were finished, he asked for the make, model, and license plate number of the getaway car.

"You'll have them as soon as I'm released," I said.

De Vroom left without providing any closure on our potential working relationship or my case. An hour later the fresh-faced kid who'd brought me to my cell came back and let me out. Another cop returned my bag, asked me to verify its contents, and made me sign a piece of paper confirming that all my personal possessions were still there. Afterwards, De Vroom brought me over to a waiting area near the front entrance to the station.

"The prosecutor's office," he said, "has decided that the people of Amsterdam would be served best by not investing the resources necessary to pursue the charges against you."

"Wonderful," I said.

He glared at me. His matinee idol looks notwithstanding, I wondered how he ever got a date in a town filled with strong Dutch women who could kick his smug ass up and down the canals. Then he smiled and my question was answered. With his looks, naturally, and his confidence.

He handed me a business card. "You can reach me day and night. I was hoping to get one of yours. With a few extra numbers on it, if you know what I mean."

I pulled out my own card and asked him if I could borrow a pen. He produced a black Montegrappa fountain pen with small skulls along the shaft and a big one on the cap. He was a stylish bastard. I had to give him that.

I wrote on the back of my card: "blue Porsche Macan Turbo. NL # RZ – DV – 99." Then I handed him the card and lowered my voice. "Will you call me with the owner's name?"

He snatched the card and read what I'd written. "Better if you call me," he said.

He didn't offer to get me a taxi, and I didn't want to stay in the police station a second longer, so I left without saying another word.

I wasn't sure exactly how long of a walk it was to my hotel, but I figured my smart phone would guide me. As it turned out, I didn't need any technological assistance. A Mercedes-Benz sedan was idling a few cars lengths away from the entrance to the station. A man got out of the front passenger seat and opened the rear passenger seat door.

Simmy Simeonovich poked his head out and motioned for me to come over. It was more a wave than a curled finger, something akin to what the Pope of Rome does when he's saying hello to several million bystanders.

I crossed the street, frustrated, embarrassed, and livid with him. *How the hell did he know I'd rented a window prostitute's office in the first place? Was he having me followed from the moment he'd hired me? If so, why?*

I stopped beside the car and faced him.

"Tonight confirms something I suspected about you," Simmy said.

I glared at him. "What's that?"

"Green really is your best color."

CHAPTER 5

I could tell our dynamic had changed as soon as I got in Simmy's car. He didn't smile at me, though that wasn't unusual. He rarely smiled. I assumed that was a prerequisite to a thriving business-man's survival in Russia. A man awash in riches shouldn't appear happy when most of his fellow countrymen barely make a living and are the subjects of a police state. Still, I usually spied mischief in the curl of his lip or a twinkle in his eye. Tonight, he looked straight ahead at the seat rest in front of him as though it con-tained a television monitor. But it didn't.

His driver stepped out of the vehicle and joined the other bodyguard outside without any prompting. A moment of dread seized me as I imagined Simmy firing and severing all contact with me. But then I reminded myself that I could be very persuasive and that I had some questions of my own for him.

"How are you?" he said, without looking at me.

"Never better."

"Did they treat you like professionals?"

"Sure. Just like the FSB." The FSB was the Russian federal police, the successor to the notorious KGB.

"There are some things you shouldn't joke about," he said.

"No. This is Amsterdam. Not Moscow. You can joke about anything you want. That's the definition of the free world."

Simmy rolled his eyes and shook his head. "So nice to see you, Nadia." He paused and delivered each of his next words with calculated precision. "So nice for so many people to see so much of you."

"You disapprove," I said. I was now certain he was disgusted with me, which depressed and infuriated me at the same time.

"Of what? You being arrested or posing as a prostitute?"

"You hired me. You were the one that said my performance over the last year had proven that I had investigative capabilities beyond the financial. What was it you said exactly? Oh, yes. That I have complete command of a vast arsenal that would be perfect for this case."

"And you thought that meant you should become a prostitute?"

"I was acting. I was borrowing from my arsenal, doing whatever was necessary to get the job done."

Simmy shook his head, looking as though he were lost in space. "There are some things a woman should never do. A Russian woman ... a European lady. I can't imagine any of the fine ladies I know doing such a thing."

"Can you imagine any of the fine Russian ladies you know solving this murder?"

He glanced at me, then cocked his head at angle and raised his eyebrows, as though admitting I had a point.

"You said it yourself," I said. "The mystery lover was the only lead I had. There was no other way to find him. A woman in green had to be in that window. Otherwise he would have kept moving. And with all the men walking along the streets of *De Wallen*, I couldn't assume I I'd be able to pick him out of the crowd by standing to the side and watching."

"What did the police charge you with?"

"Nothing. There are no charges. I'm back on the case. In fact, I never left it."

"Yes, but I watched them shackle your wrists. They put handcuffs on you. I saw you get arrested. They had to charge you with something."

"Lying. Solicitation. Fraternizing with Russians on Dutch soil. You know, the usual tourist misunderstandings."

"Why did they release you? Did you share something pertaining to our case? Do you know something?"

I didn't want Simmy to know I was cooperating with the police because he was obsessed with secrecy. He'd requested I keep all matters pertaining to the case confidential. The deceased girl's mother was a childhood friend of his.

"Why are you here in the first place?" I said.

"I hate it when you answer a question with a question."

"Of course you do. You're used to people giving you the answer you want in hopes being agreeable will somehow make them richer. How did you know I was in the window?"

Simmy seemed to consider his words carefully. "I didn't. One of my men has been watching it since the girl's death."

"Why?"

"It's where Iskra worked. It seemed the wise thing to do."

"Why didn't you tell me this?"

Simmy shrugged. "I didn't see how it would conflict with your efforts."

"That doesn't answer my question."

This time he glared at me. His frosty stare answered the question. He was used to informing people at his own discretion.

"That's not acceptable," I said. "I can't run an investigation if you're running one at the same time. Everything to do with this case must go through me. Now, do you want to continue in that spirit, or do you want to drop me off at the hotel and take over yourself?"

Always meet strength with strength when you have the advantage. I knew I still had the advantage. He wouldn't have hired me if he thought he could solve the murder himself. I may have embarrassed or disappointed him with my methods, but he still needed me. Otherwise we wouldn't have been talking. He would have fired me already.

"You don't have to impress me with your chutzpah, Nadia. I know you're shameless and I know you're bold. I'm sure that's part of your allure, although I'm not always sure why. Did it occur to you to ask me for help?"

"Help? Me?"

"Yes. Help. You could have borrowed one of my men and had him prepared to track the so-called mystery lover if he ran from your door, as it turned out he did."

"Unfortunately, as you know, that's my tragic flaw."

"I beg your pardon?"

"My arsenal only functions if I'm working alone."

"Ah, yes. Nadia, brave and solitary warrior. In the future you may want to remember that your vast arsenal is only valuable if you produce results."

"Who said I didn't get any results tonight?"

He shot me a glance. "Do you do know something I don't?"

I shook my head and sighed for effect. "I'm sorry," I said. "This is just not going to work."

"Why won't this work?" he said.

"Because you're lying to me again."

He appeared dumbfounded. "I'm lying to you?"

"You're withholding information."

He turned stoic again, as though he considered withholding information far less egregious a sin than an outright lie. Most businessmen did. So had my deceased ex-husband. He'd been the dreamboat Ukrainian-American catch. We'd been the toast of the community and my mother the source of all its envy, and neither she nor I, his accommodating Catholic victim, wanted to contemplate that he might have been withholding information.

"Your bodyguard let you know I was in the window," I said. "The three of you saw me go after the mystery lover. One of your bodyguards must have followed me, but he never got close enough to see the getaway car. Am I right?"

Simmy shrugged. "So what?"

"So what? Simmy, we've been around the world together on business, yours and mine. We dug up a grave outside of Chornobyl to see if the bones of a young girl were inside. I thought we'd developed a certain level of trust between us. But now you're being the oligarch all over again, not telling me you'd staked out Iskra's office, and not telling me that one of your men followed me when I gave chase. Why are you keeping all this stuff from me?"

He stared at me intently, then closed his eyes, and shook his head. "Ay-yah-yay. You're right." He reached over and squeezed my hand.

I waited for the customary bolt of electricity to run through me but it didn't.

"I'm sorry," he said. "I haven't been myself lately."

"The sanctions?" I said.

The United States and Europe were continuing to ramp up economic penalties against Russian businessmen as punishment for President Valery Putler's tacit war in Ukraine.

"Western banks froze the assets of three of the President's closest allies yesterday. And a friend of mine with a Gulfstream jet was told he would no longer receive parts or service from the company, and that his pilots would not be allowed to use the Gulfstream navigation system."

"I'd tell you I'm sorry, except you know that I'm not."

I cherished my ancestral Ukrainian heritage. Which made my relationship with a Russian oligarch all the more unlikely and complicated.

"And that's not the worst part," Simmy said. "One of my closest friends — a man of Russian industry — was stupid enough to complain to the press about our President. The reporter must have gotten him at the absolute wrong moment. The easiest way for a successful Russian businessman to cease being successful is to criticize the President. Rule number one for men such as us — stay out of politics. And it does me no good that it's a friend of mine who's commenting on exactly that — politics. The company you keep in Russia is almost as important as the palms you grease."

I could sense his exasperation and an uncharacteristic helplessness. He couldn't control what his friend said, or how Putler reacted. Yet based on Simmy's comments, both could alter his life quickly and profoundly. That was enough to frustrate any human being, but for an oligarch who'd built his empire with his bare hands and was used to controlling his own destiny, it had to be mind-numbing.

I knew of only one way to give my client some comfort, and that was to keep him informed and get the job done.

"The getaway car was a Porsche Macan," I said. "Metallic Blue." I gave him the license plate number, too.

He sighed with relief, more than my revelation deserved. Iskra's mother really was a close friend of his, I thought.

"I'll make some inquiries," he said. "In the meantime, Iskra's mother told me that her husband has overcome his grief enough to speak with you now."

That was good news. The mother, a colonel in the Salvation Army, had been away in Rotterdam on business the day Iskra died. The father had gone over to visit his daughter and found her crucified on a wall in her bedroom.

"Did you talk to him?" I said.

"That's not realistic."

"Why?"

"He doesn't like me for some reason."

"How close were you with Iskra's mother?"

"She was a girlfriend of mine in what feels like a prior life. Today, she's just an old friend. Are you hungry?"

I glanced at my watch. "It's two-forty-five in the morning. Everything's closed in Amsterdam."

"Not everything. The Burger Bar is open. I can offer you black angus or Wagyu beef."

"I had my mind on a nice Riesling, Thai food, and sea salt caramel chocolates."

"Then I cannot help you."

I snapped my head to the right and stared out the passenger side window so as not to betray the magnitude of my disappointment. In the past he would have never taken no for an answer. He would have had his driver haul ass to the Burger Bar and insisted on putting nutrition inside me. It was the care and attention he lavished on me without ever making an inappropriate remark that had endeared him to me. I was the irreverent American analyst who challenged him and refused to kiss his self-styled ring, and he seemed to enjoy my company.

Until tonight. Something had changed Simmy's attitude toward me. It might have been my bikini-clad walk through *De Wallen*, fear that the sanctions would hit him next, or something beyond my comprehension. But for now, at least, I was merely a vendor providing a service.

If I'd been focused, I might have realized the truth then, that solving Iskra's murder was merely the beginning of my true assignment for Simmy, a prerequisite to achieving his real objective, which was linked to the Russian girl's murder in the most extraordinary way. If I hadn't been distracted by my attraction to him I might have deduced that finding Iskra's killer would only put me and all I held dear in even greater danger. But I was distracted, by money and power and all that one of the richest men in the world could offer, as a client, friend, and in my most private fantasies, an even more intimate companion.

The bodyguards re-entered the car and the driver took off toward my hotel. I sat quietly beside Simmy. As the minutes passed, I shifted closer to the window away from him. Memo to oligarch: none of the American men I'd known through the years would insult a woman by telling her she was classless to her face. Rather than sulk, however, I reminded myself of a certain philosophy that had served me well since I'd learned it in PLAST, the Ukrainian girl scouts.

When injured or in pain, don't whine. Keep your mouth shut and your eyes open. Put one foot forward toward your destination, drag the other one ahead of it and repeat.

A murderer was walking the streets out there, perhaps still in Amsterdam. Some pretty boy had run away from me and impeded my investigation.

I was going to find him.

CHAPTER 6

Breakfast came with the room at my hotel, and they offered a royal buffet and eggs to order. This morning I ignored the magnetic pull of the chocolate croissant basket, the aged cheeses, and the fresh squeezed juices, and settled for an egg white omelet and four slices of cucumber. I still had my mind set on Thai food and sea salt caramel, and I was determined to wait until at least a partial celebration was in order.

I left De Vroom three messages before noon for him to call me back. He didn't. I was sure he'd traced the license plate by now. With each passing hour, I imagined the mystery lover slipping further from my grasp. He was no fool. He'd bolted as soon as he'd seen me in Iskra's office. He'd kept his cool on the sidewalk and he'd had a car waiting for him at a designated spot. The car was the latest Porsche model, priced at over one hundred thousand euro. The mystery lover was either loaded or had access to the wealth of his family or friends. He'd sat in the back of the Macan even though the front passenger seat had been empty, suggesting he might have had a driver. If he were fearful of being discovered or had another motive to leave town, I suspected he had the means with which to disappear quickly and effectively. My fear was that he was already gone.

In the absence of progress on that front, I turned my attention to something within my control. Iskra Romanova had lived in an apartment in the sleek and sexy *Jordaan* area in West Amsterdam. The northern part of *Jordaan* boasted a quaint row of shops and restaurants along *Haarlemmerstraat*, less than a mile's walk from my hotel. I called and asked Iskra's father, George Romanov, to meet me for lunch. He sounded curt and reluctant on the phone, but he finally agreed.

The phrase *"Stout!"* was a Dutch term used in reference to people who were misbehaving or calling attention to themselves. In this case, it was also the name of a cute café in *Jordaan* favored by thirty-somethings, and one of the few establishments in *Jordaan* that was open for lunch. I thought the restaurant's name was perfect for my agenda in a contrarian way, as I was intent on behaving properly and calling no attention to myself. I feared Iskra's father was more likely to do the restaurant's name justice, given his unfriendly vibe on the phone. I pictured the prototypical ruddy Russian who drank the savings his wife didn't spend on clothes she should have never been seen wearing.

How wrong I was.

I took a table on the elevated floor in the back of the restaurant. I counted fifteen couples eating lunch, and when Romanov stepped inside, all eyes went to him. He looked like a Russian athlete who'd never stopped training or crying after being left off the Olympic team twenty-five years ago. His face was a slum crammed with lines, pits, and pock marks where shadows grew and tears collected. His green suede jacket gathered at the tiniest waist and looked like a cobra's hood around his torso. Above the neck, he seemed destined for assisted living. Below the neck, he appeared competition-ready.

He barely looked at me when he muttered hello, and his expression could have frozen the melted wax beneath the candle at our table. I detected a mixture of grief and anger so palpable I felt at risk of being assaulted if I said the wrong thing.

"Let's get one thing straight," he said, in Russian. "I'm only here because my wife insisted. I'm here for my daughter. She said you come highly recommended by that egomaniac-friend of hers. If it weren't for my Iskra and how desperately I seek justice for her murder, I would never be seen talking with you."

"Why is that, Mr. Romanov?" I said.

"Because you're an American whore."

His charm and subtlety caught me by surprise. I assumed we shared the same objective, which meant our relationship would be civil. Obviously that wasn't going to be the case. I managed a big smile, in keeping with the theme of maintaining a contrarian disposition while dining in an establishment called Stout!

"I'm not sure what you mean when you say I'm a whore," I said.

He shrugged as though I'd asked him to explain why borsch was red. "You're the product of a decaying society with no morals. American women are so revolting, they are so willing to spread their legs for anyone with money that their own men come to Russia and Ukraine to look for wives, to find women with virtue and grace. Take you, for example. My wife told me you rented yourself out as a prostitute last night. What self-respecting woman would do such a thing under any circumstances? Only a woman for whom it comes naturally. In other words, only a whore. You, Miss Tesla, are the lowest form of life from the lowest society on this planet. You are an American whore."

His words started a fire inside me, and the implication that Simmy had told his wife about my methods in *De Wallen* only served to stoke them. I let the flames subside for a few seconds. Then I licked my lips and gave him my own shrug.

"Well, I'm insulted, Mr. Romanov. I'm not going to pretend otherwise. I don't know of any other woman who would have posed as a prostitute in an Amsterdam window to find your daughter's killer, and I'm certain I was the only American working *De Wallen* last night. So please don't insult me by calling me an American whore. I'm not an American whore."

"Then what are you?"

"I'm *the* American whore."

Romanov blinked several times as though not believing what he'd heard me say.

"I'm *the* American whore. I'm the one. I'm the one that's going to find the bastard who drove screws through your daughter's hands and feet. I'm the one that's going to find out who snuffed out your little girl's life by letting her bleed to death." I bared my teeth. "So the next time you decide to call me names, get it right, my self-indulgent Russian friend."

Romanov appeared ready to launch himself across the table. "How dare you …"

A petite waitress with hesitant eyes had walked up to our table without my realizing it. She asked if we wanted something to drink. The question snapped Romanov out of his rage. He settled back in his seat like a coronary patient who realized he shouldn't let his blood pressure rise. He ordered coffee. I chose still water. When she asked us if we knew what we wanted to eat, Romanov glanced at the menu.

"Yoghurt, granola, wolfberries," he said.

The waitress noted his selection on her pad and turned to me.

I had no idea what wolfberries were but I liked the sound of them. Plus the insatiable hunger in my stomach had died the moment Romanov had criticized America.

"Just the wolfberries," I said.

The waitress started to write and stopped. She raised her eyebrows. "Just the wolfberries?"

"That's right. Just the wolfberries."

She jotted my order down, slipped her pencil behind her ear and left.

Romanov studied me with a condescending smile. "You are such Nazis."

That was a new one. "I beg your pardon?"

"First there was Napoleon, then Hitler, and now there's America. You want to corrupt the entire world for the sake of your own interests. That's why you fight the subversive war against Russia, trying to poison our youth with your message of homosexuality and pedophilia."

"Excuse me?"

"And when our president stands up to your imperialist ways – who are you to tell Russians how to manage their region – you punish our country with economic sanctions. The only question is how long it will take for your society to crumble. You have no family values, you have no childbirth, you have no future."

It sounded to me as though Romanov's cable television was set permanently to the Russian channel, except I'd never heard the bit about pedophilia.

"That's not the question, Mr. Romanov." I softened my voice so it was barely audible. "The question is are you going to help your daughter get justice, or am I on my own?" I shifted in my seat and placed my leg in the aisle as though I were preparing to leave.

Romanov looked away as though contemplating whether he wanted to answer my question or vanish before his yogurt arrived. He looked back and forth into space and at me, and exhaled in one long, massive breath. He didn't look particularly relieved, just fortified enough to converse with the American whore.

"Growing up in Russia, she was a perfect child," he said. "I was an alternate on the Russian national diving team so I had certain privileges. She went to good schools. She painted, studied ballet, and was a member of *Nashi*."

"*Nashi*?" The word meant "ours."

"It's a grass roots organization of young people who love Russia. President Putler started it after the Orange Revolution in Ukraine to make sure that subversive American interests never manipulated the people of Russia into doing the same."

Of course, I thought. Whenever any country did something that threatened Putler's expanding empire, he blamed America. "What did Iskra do for *Nashi*?"

Romanov chose his words carefully, the way a man does when's trying to withhold information. "She organized rallies ... created internet sites ... campaigned for politicians and the like. She was a lovely child."

"And then?"

"And then we moved here."

"When was that?"

"Twelve years ago."

"Why did you move here? You seem to love Russia."

"Of course I love Russia, just as I'm sure you love that decrepit pit you call home." Once again, Romanov paused to consider his answer. "It was time to leave. For business reasons."

That meant he probably had to leave Russia to avoid prosecution for some offense, real or imaginary. This suggested he'd fallen out of favor with the people in the Kremlin, who may have been prepared to support his competitors' attempt to have him jailed, or were intent on subduing him themselves.

I was curious to know more, but I knew better than to pry into his business affairs. Tap a Russian's heart, and it might come pouring out. Inveigle yourself in his business affairs and he might give you an up-close and personal tour of his company's waste disposal equipment.

"How old was Iskra when you moved here?" I said.

Romanov thought about the question. "I'd say she was about nine or ten. She was a good student. When she turned seventeen, she was accepted into the modern theatre dance program at the Amsterdam School of the Arts. Her mother and I were very proud. We rented an apartment for her and gave her space. We kept our distance even though we live close by in *Oud-Zuid* – old South Amsterdam. Her mother insisted we not interfere in her life. I knew it was a mistake. She fell in with a bunch of liberal types at school and became an experimental child." He looked at me and nodded. "Probably just like you."

"How so?" I said. The only thing I'd ever experimented with outside of school was a microscope my parents gave me for my ninth birthday.

"Sex, drugs, rock and roll. It was all born in America, wasn't it?"

"Rock and roll, I think so. The other two may pre-date my decrepit homeland. I know this is a sensitive topic, but I have to ask you. How long did she work a window in *De Wallen*?"

"Spare me your false sympathy. You're a mercenary. Act like one."

"How long had Iskra been working as a prostitute?"

"Not long. Three months. She worked part-time, weekends only."

"Did you know about this from the start?" I said.

"No."

"How did you find out?"

He considered the question. "The second worst way possible."

I made the obvious deduction. "A friend?"

He shrugged. "We asked her to stop, we begged her ... I threatened to cut off all financial support but she said she didn't care. She said she wanted to make her own money and this was something she wanted to do. That if other girls from Russian were doing it, she could, too." Romanov shook his head.

"And the mystery lover wasn't her only customer?"

"I wish," he said.

"Did Iskra have a boyfriend?"

Romanov's eyes narrowed to slits. "Obviously she had a boyfriend. That was the reason you prostituted yourself—"

"I don't mean the mystery boyfriend, I mean, was there anyone else?"

He shook his head.

"There had to be other boyfriends."

"There were many boys," he said softly, "and a few men. But she never brought anyone to our house for dinner. If there had been someone serious, she would have brought him to dinner. Do you have leads on the identity of this mystery lover?"

"I'm working on it. Are you conducting any kind of inquiry of your own? Because that would not be helpful ..."

"The police warned me to stay away, and these days, a Russian in Amsterdam must listen to the police. Besides, Simeonovich has insisted to my wife that you will get to the bottom of this. And regardless of how much of a hypocrite he is – if a hand were to fall on his shoulder, it would release a mountain of dirt from beneath his Brioni suits – I have never known him to give compliments where they are not deserved."

"I agree."

Romanov nodded hopefully. "That you will get to the bottom of this?"

"That he doesn't give compliments. Do you have any enemies that might have done this?"

"I sold my business when I left Russia. There is no reason for anyone to hate me. Besides, if a Russian wanted to get even over something that happened in the distant past, he'd come after me first." He paused and looked me over. "Your last name, Tesla. What is the ethnic origin?"

"My parents were full-blooded Ukrainians."

I braced myself for a derogatory response, but instead the sun burst on his face.

"Ukrainian? Why, that is fantastic," he said.

"Why is that fantastic?"

"Because that means you're a full-blooded Russian, too."

The temperature in *Stout!* seemed to rise. "I ... I don't understand. I told you my parents were Ukrainian."

He shrugged good-naturedly, not a patronizing or condescending note about him.

"There's no such thing as Ukraine and there are no such people as Ukrainians," he said. "That's just some senseless nonsense created by a few self-styled Nazis near Poland. This is great news. The investigator from America is actually Russian. I see why Simeonovich thinks so much of you. He may be a genius after all."

If my brother, Marko, were here, he would have short-circuited, had a stroke, and fallen to his death. His demise would have been a function of not being able to decide whether to stab Romanov in the eye with his fork, or try to spoon it out and force it down his throat.

The waitress brought our food. Romanov spooned his yoghurt with zest and enthusiasm. I eyed my spoon with newfound fascination, and ate my wolfberries one at a time to make my meal last. I even calmed myself down enough to chew a few of them.

When we were done, Romanov insisted on paying the bill. I didn't object. Instead I let him impress me with his gentlemanly ways.

Then I countered with my own insistence.

I demanded he take the American whore with the Russian bloodlines to the place she wanted to go more than any other.

I insisted he take me to the scene of the crime.

CHAPTER 7

We were buddies now, the dead girl's charming father and I. Romanov actually had the nerve to open a gap in his elbow for my arm so we could walk to Iskra's hotel like old friends or new lovers headed for a café in Prague. I took him up on his offer and walked arm-in-arm with him to further earn his trust to help my investigation. Never had I been happier to be snuggled close to a man who'd called me trash. Humility was an indispensible weapon in the arsenal that was going to lead me to the pretty boy who had eluded my chase. It was also one of the hardest weapons to deploy because when you needed it the most you wanted it the least.

Romanov led me to a row of houses packed wall-to-wall. A bell-shaped gable topped the building that contained Iskra's apartment. A lattice of iron rods was strapped to each side of the house.

"To keep it upright," Romanov said, when he noticed I was staring at the rods. "The houses in Jordaan were built on thousands of logs. They were pounded into the ground because it's so wet. If you look closely, you can see the house is leaning a little bit to the right. Without support, it would eventually crumble. I told my wife this was an unstable place for our daughter to live. But my wife only listens when she's speaking."

We took the stairs to the second floor. The police had cordoned off the door to the apartment with red and white tape featuring the words "*Politie – NIET BETREDEN*." I remembered what Romanov had said about needing to behave himself in Amsterdam but evidently his interpretation of my ethnic heritage had unleashed his machismo. He ripped the tape from one side of the door frame like a matador snapping his cape, not worrying about whether he could re-attach it later. Then he took out his key and unlocked the door. The door jam and lock appeared in perfect condition.

"When you got here that day," I said, "was the door open?"

"It was closed but unlocked."

"And the windows?"

"The big windows in the living room can't be opened. The side windows in the bathroom and bedroom were locked from the inside."

"So whoever killed her knew her."

"I wouldn't know what the police are thinking. Maybe if I was Dutch they'd keep me informed."

Romanov opened the door. The apartment opened into a living room which led to a kitchen in an open floor plan. Two interior doors stood open along the wall on the left. I could see the edge of a bed in one room, and bathroom tile on the floor of the other.

"Who else has a key?" I said.

"Besides Iskra? My wife and I have a key."

Black powder stains revealed latent fingerprints on the walls, chairs and tables, and built-in cabinetry. Even from a distance I could see them all over the kitchen countertops. Other than the powder stains, however, the apartment was surprisingly well-organized given it had belonged to a twenty-something single girl.

"Did Iskra have a cleaning lady?" I said.

"Yes. An old Indonesian woman. I'm sure she had a key, too."

"Who else?"

He shrugged. "A man. A boy. Ten men. I have no way of knowing. Like I said, we gave her space."

The furniture was sleek, modern Dutch, not dissimilar to a Scandinavian design but more whimsical, with more curvaceous and lacquered finishes. Film and theater posters with dance themes hung on the walls. The kitchen gleamed apart from the print marks. I pulled my sleeve over my fingers and opened the fridge. A tray full of energy drinks, half a dozen yogurts, a jar of pickled herring, milk, pineapple juice, a huge bar of Tony's Milk Chocolate, and ten bottles of beer filled the shelves. The beer was a brand called Brugse Zot. From Belgium.

I closed the refrigerator door and studied the kitchen. The more I looked around, the more I wondered how I'd had the nerve to take this assignment. I'd told myself that the investigation of a crime was a matter of logic and common sense, that my forensic financial skills would translate. But now that I was visiting an actual crime scene, my inexperience and uncertainty asserted themselves. I feared Romanov would sense my indecision, detect my incompetence, and label me a fraud any moment.

As it turned out, he had his own issues.

"I ... I can't go in there with you," he said.

He stood at the entry to the kitchen, arms wrapped around his chest, eyes pointed diagonally toward the floor like a socially awkward teen. Up until this point, he'd been a type A personality, the king of eye contact.

I knew he was referring to the bedroom because I knew that's where Iskra had been killed. I knew what he was talking about because I felt the same dread in the pit of my own stomach. I wasn't sure if I was ready to see the room myself, yet there were my feet moving toward it with morbid anticipation. The discovery of fraud, embezzlement or an undervalued investment opportunity had always invigorated me. The moment of discovery – that instant when numbers leapt off a financial statement and transformed themselves into a firm conclusion – was the juice that fueled countless hours of labor. My walk toward the bedroom, however, galvanized my senses even more dramatically.

Light spilled through sheer curtains covering the window on the right side of the room. Streaks and splashes of blood in the shape of a wide-bodied cross marred the center of the opposite wall. The center area below the place where her Iskra's pubic region would have rested contained the most blood. In fact, so much blood had spilled from her body that the wallboard appeared black. The image of a man hacking away at Iskra's torso flashed before me. I suffered a wave of nausea.

The four points of crucifixion defined the upper and lower boundaries of the blood-stained canvas. The area of the wall surrounding the screw holes were also stained black. I walked around the bed to get a close-up look. The light-colored hardwood floor looked more like redwood as I approached the place of crucifixion.

The crime could have been a random act of violence, but given Iskra had most likely known her killer I doubted it. I wondered what kind of passion had inspired such a level of hate, gazed at the wall and wondered what else I could deduce that could be of value. As is so often the case with company analyses, I saw nothing. But I didn't allow frustration to overwhelm me. Instead I stood there staring at the blood-splattered wall, telling myself over-and-over again that patience was a prerequisite to success. This, in turn, relaxed me and kept my mind straight.

Still, nothing came to me.

"Are you okay in there?" Romanov said.

I told him I was fine and that I would be out in a moment. I decided to rest my eyes and divert my focus. I looked around the rest of the bedroom. Two pillows, stacked one on top of the other, contained indentations of a human head. The comforter, similarly matted in the shape of a human being, also remained untouched. There were no electronic devices in the room, no computer, phone, or music playing devices. The police might have removed them for analysis if they'd been here, I thought.

A closet contained an assortment of clothes and boxes on a shelf. I didn't reach for any of the boxes, nor did I rifle through the bureau beside the window opposite the wall of death. If there had been anything of interest in either of those places, the police would have secured it as evidence by now. I didn't delude myself into thinking I'd find some clue the police might have overlooked. My forte was the interpretation of that which was visible.

The bureau also contained a collection of pictures, each standing upright in frames of various sizes. Most of them featured Iskra alone, with female friends or her family. One of the family pictures, the size of a playing card, included Iskra, her parents, and a nerdy-looking boy in glasses. Iskra and the boy looked like young teens in the picture.

I removed some tissue from my bag and used it to avoid contaminating the frames with my fingertips. Then I carried the photo into the living room and showed it to Romanov.

"Who's this boy?" I said.

He narrowed his eyes and studied the picture. It was the first time I'd looked at Romanov since I'd gone into the bedroom, and his face had turned ashen in the interim. He looked as though he was fading in proportion to the time I spent at the crime scene, and if we remained in the apartment another hour, he might die from the stress.

"That's just Sasha." Romanov shook his head as though he were irrelevant. "Friend of the family. Sasha's parents moved here before we did. I knew her father forever. He and Iskra were friends."

"Just friends?"

He cracked a weary grin as though the prospect of them being romantically linked was a joke. "Yes, just friends. Sasha is a good boy, but he's Sasha, you understand—"

Feet clattered outside the door.

De Vroom burst into the room. Another man in a suit and two uniformed cops followed. De Vroom looked like a completely different human being from the one who'd interviewed me in jail. Gone was the smug look of a calculating cop intent on getting the information he wanted. In its place was fury.

"What are you doing here?" he said.

"This woman is a friend of the family," Romanov said in decent English. "She's here at my request."

"Your request?" De Vroom said. "You have no business being here either. This is a crime scene. When you took down that tape, you broke the law."

Romanov brought his wrists together and offered them to DeVroom. "Go ahead, then. Arrest a grieving father. After all, I'm Russian, so you want to prosecute me for something, don't you?"

De Vroom averted Romanov's eyes, turned to me, and ripped the frame out of my hands. "And this is evidence in a murder investigation." He glanced at the picture, looked at both of us as though we deserved the firing squad, and handed the picture back to his colleague. "You," he said, pointing at me, "outside. Now."

He insisted I go down the stairs first. I could feel him so close behind me I was afraid he'd step on the back of my shoe.

We exited the apartment building. The sight of the canal and the blue sky above would have been welcome relief if De Vroom hadn't been with me.

"Did you run that license plate?" I said.

"You will cease all investigations into this case immediately. You will leave Amsterdam at once. If I find you nosing around the murder of Iskra Romanova one more time, we'll forget about our arrangement. I'll press charges against you for obstructing justice, illegal prostitution, and being a menace to the Netherlands. I'll have you deported, banned, and ex-communicated from whatever godforsaken church accepts you as a member."

He was hurling so many bombs at me I had to take a second to make sure he was done. Only then did I speak.

"Yeah, but did you run that plate?" I said.

His cheeks puffed up so much he actually stopped being handsome for a moment. Then he took a deep breath and lowered his voice to a whisper, so gentle and infused with such genuine-sounding concern that I lost my breath.

"For your own safety, Nadia," he said. It was the first time he'd ever used my Christian name, and it put fear in my heart. "You must stop this now. You must leave Amsterdam now."

With that he turned and marched back up stairs and into the apartment building. When the door shut behind him, I knew not to follow him back inside. I knew not to wait for Romanov. If De Vroom saw me waiting for him, that alone could set him off into following up on his threat, and I couldn't take that risk.

I headed back along the canal toward my hotel instead. With each step, De Vroom's heartfelt warning left a deeper impression on me. He had run the plate. Perhaps the owner of the Porsche Macan was so dangerous that my life would be in jeopardy if I went near him. I thought of the crime lords who controlled the sex and drug trades in Amsterdam and what they might be capable of doing to protect their businesses. After De Vroom's warning, only an addict would pursue this case. Only a woman with a compulsive need to prove herself would dare continue.

And as I looked onto the canal and wondered if I were such a person, the obvious hit me. It hit me straight on, like a six-inch screw that penetrated paint and sheet-rock and sank deep into wood on the first try.

A spare anchor on a boat moored beside the road on the edge of the canal reminded me of the help I'd once given my father. He'd needed to hang a Ukrainian-Catholic cross, the kind with three bars going perpendicular to the vertical one, with the bottom one at an angle. This particular cross was made of iron and required an anchor — a wall anchor. The teeth of the wall anchor gripped the sheet rock and kept the wallboard from crumbling under the heavy weight. Wall anchors required large holes and their removal left visible gashes in the sheet rock.

The holes in the wall where Iskra had been crucified had been perfect, round holes. That meant the screws had hit the wood that supported the wallboard perfectly. The wood behind the wallboard usually consisted of two-inch by four-inch studs spaced intermittently. The only way to know the exact location of the two-by-fours was by using a stud-finder, which often employed a magnet to detect the screws that secured the sheetrock to the wood.

Iskra's killer had not only brought screws and a driver-drill to the crime scene, he'd brought a stud finder, too. Her killing had been a pre-meditated murder planned with precision. My suspicion was that the killer was a friend, that Iskra had let him in, and that he'd executed a plan he'd imagined for days, weeks, or even months. He'd dreamed about driving the screws precisely where they needed to go for her bodyweight to be supported, relished the thought of slicing her feminine body parts from the rest of her body with a knife. And he'd probably had help. It would have been difficult for one man to hold the body and drive the screws into the wood.

This was a crime of passion and a cold-blooded killing.

I pulled out my cell phone and called Simmy.

I needed the name and address of the owner of that damn car.

CHAPTER 8

To get the name and address of the owner of the blue Porsche Macan Turbo that had whisked the mystery lover to safety, I needed to deploy humility for the second time in an hour. That was bordering on dangerous behavior, because a woman must maintain a sliver of ego or risk becoming a door mat for family, friends, clients and especially, would-be lovers. The probability that Simmy would ever be the latter had dropped faster than De Vroom had transformed himself into the prince of darkness. Still, a woman never stops dreaming, even about outcomes she's not entirely sure she wants – Ukrainians and Russians don't always mix easily or well.

I called Simmy on his cell phone, a number only six people possessed: his assistant, ex-wife, two children, the coach of his professional soccer team, and I. Or so he'd told me.

I asked him if he'd traced the plate.

"What happened to your fatal flaw?" he said.

"You mean the one where my vast arsenal is effective only if I work alone?"

"No. The one where you're arrogant enough to allow yourself to believe it."

"It's trumped by one of my greatest virtues."

"Really? I don't think I remember this virtue. Refresh my memory."

"Sure," I said. "No problem. It's the one where I get the job done no matter what."

"Oh, yes. That one. I knew there was something about you that I liked. As a matter of fact I just received some information from my man in Brussels. I was about to call you. You have a pen, pencil, or a needle to draw some blood?"

"I used my needle to thread my way into the crime scene but I've got my trusty lipstick. Go ahead."

He gave me an address in Bruges that belonged to a woman by the name of Sarah Dumont. I made a note of it on my mobile phone.

"Do you have a phone number?" I said.

"Aren't you the detective?"

"Weren't you the one who said I should ask for help when I need it?"

"No, I don't have a phone number. There's no trace of this woman other than her name on that motor vehicle registration. Which is, of course, impossible."

"She's probably the boy's mother. The odds are low she'd be forthcoming over the phone." I didn't bother to finish up my thought process, as I was sure Simmy knew where I was leading.

"Have you been to Bruges?" he said.

I remembered pictures of a medieval city that looked like a theme park but was actually the real deal.

"No."

"Then there's something you should be aware of before you go and try to blend in."

"What's that?" I said.

"The local authorities frown on prostitution."

I cringed. What a disappointment. I wondered why I'd ever been attracted to him. "Thank you for confirming my theory."

"Oh, yes?" His tone acquired an edge. He sounded as though he were picking a fight. "What theory?"

"The bigger the bucks, the badder the revelations."

I ended the call before he could answer, and then cursed at myself. I had to take three deep breaths just to recover. He was a paying client. In fact, he was my most important paying client. I'd indulged my emotions which meant I was not on top of my game. This realization sobered me up. I had no choice but to produce results or my entire livelihood would be threatened. One bad recommendation from my most important client would ruin me.

I went back to the hotel and made arrangements for a quick trip to Bruges. A little over an hour later I hopped on a Thalys high-speed train to Brussels, switched to a Belgian local, and arrived in Bruges just before 7:00 p.m. I took a taxi to the Hotel Dukes' Palace, checked in and got a map to get myself acclimated.

A promotional pamphlet for the Bruges Beer Museum in the hotel lobby reminded me of the contents of Iskra's refrigerator. Among them were four bottles of a Bruges beer, not the most common selection in a country that produced Heineken, Grolsch, and Amstel. That suggested she'd acquired a taste for it coincidentally, or at the suggestion of her mystery lover. I suspected it was the latter. Objectivity defined the investigator's vision, but optimism greased the wheels that propelled her to the solution.

Perhaps the path to finding the solution was in Bruges.

The growling in my stomach drowned out the echo of De Vroom's ominous warning. I needed nourishment but I wanted answers even more. I had a quick chat with a courteous man at the front desk about the layout of the central square and beyond. Afterwards, he called a taxi for me. Five minutes later I was seated in the back of a Peugeot with my cell phone displaying a map of the local area.

The weary driver spoke good English. He told me Bruges was called the "Venice of the North," which was funny because that's what the cabbie in Amsterdam had said about his hometown. Both cities were built around canals, but that's where the similarities ended. Whereas Amsterdam offered a contemporary urban vibe in a historical city, Bruges looked like history itself surrounded by contemporary trappings.

The drive through the Markt and Burg areas was an exercise in medieval architectural time travel. Spotlights attached to vaulted rooftops illuminated gabled and gilded buildings from centuries past. In the background, a fourteenth century bell tower loomed with an octagonal-shaped lantern on top. There were no sword-wielding, armor-clad warriors on horseback, but the city center's authentic aura made it easy to picture them thundering around the corner. In their place, tourists ambled along winding cobblestone streets filled shoulder-to-shoulder amidst chocolate shops, boutiques, and restaurants.

The ever-present canals connected the various neighborhoods, murky waterways that disappeared now and then under the curved arches of the bridges above. Homes carved from stone or assembled with bricks faced the water. I'd travelled one hundred fifty miles but I was still surrounded by canals. If I'd been on vacation, I might have focused on their aesthetics. Nothing promotes a sense of serenity like a calm body of water. But a girl had been crucified and slaughtered in one of the Venices of the north, and my investigation of her murder had taken me to the other. Instead of beauty, I saw hidden depths, untold mysteries, and gentle black ripples that belied a stirring beneath the surface.

We drove past the city center into a calm residential neighborhood located across a canal called St. Gilles. Two miles further the driver came to a fork and stopped in front of a road that disappeared into a densely wooded area. The car's headlights provided sufficient light for me to see that the road had been recently paved. There were no cracks in the asphalt and the curbs stood firm and round above ground level.

The driver's voice fell a few octaves. "This is the address." He pointed down the road, then pulled his finger back and looked away as though he was afraid someone might have seen him.

"You mean this is a private road?" I said.

"Yes."

"And there's only one house in there?"

I spied the driver's face in the rearview mirror. His eyes bugged out. "You do not know this? I assumed you had an appointment with the owner."

"Who is the owner?" I said.

"If you don't know that, you don't belong here. And if you don't belong here, I don't want to be here."

He started to turn the car around.

"Stop." I slammed the seatback in front of me with an open palm.

The car jerked to a halt.

I pulled my wallet out and handed the driver twenty euro. "Who lives here?"

The driver glanced at the money uncertainly, as though he was almost tempted. I added another twenty. He snatched the bills from my hand.

"A very successful woman," he said. "She's a theater person, famous in the theater. You're from England. You know the type, I'm sure."

No one had ever mistaken my accent for a British one, but any confusion about my origins or anything else about me was welcome.

"Then why can't you take me in there so I can get a closer look?"

"There's a gate," he said. "There's security. It is not a place where one should go unless invited."

"Why?"

The driver rolled his eyes and gnashed his teeth as though I were exasperating him beyond the call of cabbie duty, or the benefit of forty euro. "The story around town is that the woman lived in Amsterdam for a while but there was a home invasion. A very ugly thing. They say she was lucky she survived. She moved to Bruges and built this house. There is a gate and there is security, and the men who work there have a fierce reputation."

The cabbie's inflection suggested the bodyguards had demonstrated this ferocity.

"Oh, c'mon," I said. "Fierce reputation? This is Belgium, not the Congo. How long has she lived here?"

"A year? No. More. A year and a half. Has to be going on two."

"Have they killed anyone yet?"

"Not to my knowledge, but I have no interest in being the first one."

"Then there's no problem," I said. "People take the wrong turn, they get lost all the time, don't they? What's the worst that can happen?"

I pulled another twenty euro from my wallet, put it between thumb and forefinger, and rubbed it near his ear.

He shook his head with reluctance and grabbed the bill. Then he turned the nose of the car toward the new road and powered forward with surprising conviction, a torrent of Dutch words pouring from his lips as he did so.

As soon as he entered the road the headlights shone on a succession of signs that reminded me of the main road to Chornobyl. The entrance to the sight of Ukraine's nuclear disaster was marked with warning, hazard, and "Do Not Enter" signs. This road was no different. For a moment I wondered why the formal entrance wasn't placed at the intersection with the main road, but a mile later we rounded a bend and I understood the builder's logic.

Soft lights illuminated a gleaming silver gate. The gatehouse beside it was also contemporary, with steel beams and glass on all sides. The modern structures seemed at such odds with the character of Bruges they jarred the senses. The gate's purpose was to provide privacy for Sarah Dumont. If it had been placed at the mouth of the road, the gate would have achieved the exact opposite purpose. It would have been a magnet for attention. Still, Sarah Dumont's design skills seemed questionable at best. *Wouldn't it have been more appropriate to build something quaint in keeping with the wooded surroundings and Bruges itself?* I wondered if her choice was a function of arrogance or poor taste.

Spotlights burst with light. They obliterated our vision. The driver slammed on the brakes. The car jerked to a stop.

"This is as far as I go," the driver said. "You've seen the gate, now we go."

"Relax," I said, as much to myself as to him. I had butterflies in my stomach, but I couldn't imagine a woman could get killed for trespassing in a tourist city in Belgium. Besides, as my first boss, a transplant from Birmingham to New York City had told me on my first day at work in corporate America, a faint heart never fucked the cook.

I whipped the door open and stepped outside. "Turn the car around and wait for me here. Remember, if you leave without me, I can't give you the biggest tip I've ever given a cabbie."

I marched toward the gatehouse without further thought. Two figures moved around the periphery of the spotlights shining from either side of the gate. One appeared to be accompanied by a beast on four legs. A man shouted something in what sounded like Dutch. The words didn't register.

"Stop!"

That word definitely registered and I slowed down. But once again I invoked my training from the Ukrainian girl scouts and pushed myself to act contrary to my desires. I put one foot in front of the other at an even faster clip and headed straight toward the gate.

As I neared the gate, one of the spotlights followed me. The light blinded me so badly I had to raise my hand to shield my eyes. More shouting followed, and I became aware of a dog barking. Or perhaps it had been barking all along and I hadn't heard it over the thumping of my heart.

The light blinding me dimmed but my vision remained impaired. Purple and black images moved before me. The same two men, one holding a dog with a leash, the other a steering wheel locking mechanism. I wondered why a security guard would carry such a thing.

Both men were long and lean, and dressed in black turtlenecks and field jackets. The one without the dog barked something in Dutch at me again which I didn't understand.

"Would you give my business card to Ms. Dumont, please?" I reached into my handbag for the black leather case that held my cards—

"Stop."

I stopped moving, hand in bag.

The man with the steering wheel locking mechanism device charged me. The other one released his beast, which snarled, leaped at me and knocked me down. A bolt of pain shot up my hip as I crashed to the asphalt.

The dog climbed onto my chest and bared its teeth six inches from my face. That's when I noticed the animal's long, bushy fur, pointed ears and ferocious eyes. The animal wasn't a dog, I realized. It was a gray wolf.

The man with the device pointed the tip of his locking mechanism at my torso. When I saw its barrel I realized it wasn't a steering wheel locking device. It was some sort of fancy submachine gun built for the twenty-first century. A vision of Apple or Amazon extending their technological expertise into weapons flashed in my mind, and I wondered if the gun could put a bullet in a specific body part with a simple voice command. "Are you people out of your mind?" I said. "I'm from America, on sensitive business that involves Ms. Dumont. I have a certain reputation with the financial press. You want an international incident? I can get a Bloomberg, CNBC, or MSNBC news crew out here real easy."

I'd posed as reporter before which is why those words came to me so quickly. One of the men called off the wolf. The other helped me to my feet. They searched my bag and body with respect and efficiency. After one of them handed my bag back to me, I gave him my business card.

"Please tell Ms. Dumont that I'd like to talk to her about her son. I'm staying at the Hotel Dukes' Plaza. I'm not leaving until I speak with her, one way or another."

I glanced beyond the gatehouse before turning away to leave. My vision had adjusted enough for me to spy the small palace in the distance. It looked like a misplaced ice sculpture, a rectangular home carved from glass. In the driveway sat a gunmetal Audi coupe with flared haunches. Beside it, the metallic blue Porsche Macan Turbo. Lights shone in the house. I strongly suspected Sarah Dumont was home. The intensity of her security team's performance suggested they were guarding a person or persons, not just a building.

I walked slowly back to the taxi, playing it cool so that I didn't betray that they'd succeeded in shaking me up. Getting mugged by a wolf had a lasting effect on one's nervous system.

On the way back to the hotel, I considered the reason Sarah Dumont had chosen Bruges as her new home. I understood the obvious allure. Bruges offered quality restaurants, world-class shopping, a unique aesthetic, and access to transportation. The Brussels Airport was a two hour drive to the south, and the English Channel an hour away in the north. But it was still an odd choice, as unlikely as the type of home she'd built and the materials from which it was made. Her choice and lifestyle seemed off to me, and carried the strong whiff of someone whose money had criminal ties. This was based on my experience with the Ukrainian and Russian mafia types, whose taste tended toward the ostentatious. In this case, Ms. Dumont's choices weren't so ostentatious as they were unlikely.

As were mine. I'd taken a case whose criminal nature was beyond my area of expertise in a foreign country. With each new obstacle to overcome I became increasingly unwilling to quit or fail. I could feel the determination building inside me, like some mass between my heart and soul that could not be obliterated by anything short of a definitive solution to the crime. To arrive at that solution, I was now going to have alter my strategy.

I wasn't going to penetrate this woman's fortress to meet the pretty boy she was protecting.

I would have to wait for my mark to venture forth and pounce on her in the open.

CHAPTER 9

I was careful to resist the temptation of befriending a taxi driver. I'd succumbed to that convenience in Kyiv two years ago and it nearly got me killed. A cabbie earned my trust and sold me out to my enemy. He seduced me with his looks, intellect, and fluency in the language of my forefathers during my first trip to Ukraine. He sang me a love song, too. I romanticized my circumstances, dropped my guard, and was betrayed for my imprudence. The experience had taught me a valuable lesson.

When on the job or off it, never romanticize your circumstances.

Still, the next morning I needed a driver I could trust. I called the same cabbie who'd driven me the night before and told him I needed his services again. I figured he was perfectly qualified because he hadn't sung me any love songs and I hadn't dreamed about him, either, and those were understatements.

By six-fifteen we were parked by the side of the road beyond the fork that led to Sarah Dumont's house. The driver's beard looked like the a coat of black lacquer paint and the cabin reeked of coffee.

"Why was it necessary to come here so early?" he said.

"Because I don't know when she's going to leave the house."

"You should have asked me."

"What?" I said.

"You should have asked me about the woman's schedule."

"How would you know her schedule?"

"I don't know her schedule."

"You're confusing me," I said.

"I don't know her schedule, but I know her routine."

"She's that well-known in town that everyone knows her routine?"

"I wouldn't say that everyone knows her routine. I'd say that all sorts of people know bits and pieces about her, and in a town like Bruges, taxi drivers tend to know the sum of what all people know."

"Okay, you know more than I do. What's her routine?"

"She exercises in town on weekdays in the morning," the driver said.

"At what time?"

"That I cannot tell you."

"But you know she's home now, right?"

The driver cast a look of irritation in the rearview mirror. "No, I don't know that. How am I supposed to know where she is?"

"You said you know her routine."

"Yes," the driver barked. "When she's in town, at her home, I know her routine. But she travels much. Like I told you, she's in the theater."

We sat in the car quietly. The driver began snoring, a gnarly rasp with an impressive rhythmic consistency, like the metronome from hell. While he slept, I used my phone to search for gyms and physical fitness facilities in Bruges. The particulars of three establishments popped up. The first two had no record of a Sarah

Dumont among their clients. I fared better with the third one, a place called the Continental Gym.

"Good morning," I said, adding a German inflection to my voice to disguise myself. "My name is Monica Mulder. I'm calling on behalf of Miss Sarah Dumont. I'm her personal assistant. Ms. Dumont recently changed her phone number and I'm calling to verify you have the right one."

A more formal enterprise might have had a more experienced person manning the front desk, someone who would have asked me to give her the new number first. But this was a workout facility which meant it was defined by pace, motion, and cheap labor. Music blared in the background. A blender whirred. The girl who answered the phone told me to hang on while she looked up the number on the computer, and then promptly gave it to me.

I made a note of it, told her it was the right number, and hung up. The driver had continued snoring through my calls. I savored a victorious moment and contemplated my strategy during the next hour. My thoughts must have numbed me to the sounds of my surroundings because I never heard any motor noises until the car appeared in the fork ahead.

It was the metallic blue Porsche Macan.

I tapped the driver on the shoulder. He snapped out of his trance, cleared his throat, grasped the steering wheel and took off. I didn't have to say a single word. His awakening was the insomniac's equivalent to the way martial artists snapped to their feet without using their hands. I was so pleased with him I leaned forward and patted his shoulder twice.

"The driver is probably a policeman or ex-military ..." I said.

He grumbled under his breath. "You are not the first passenger to ask me to follow someone."

"You are full of pleasant surprises this morning and clearly one of the finest men in Bruges. Onwards, but not too closely."

The driver followed the Macan to the Continental Gym outside the city center. Sarah Dumont jumped out of the back of the SUV on her own – she didn't wait for the driver to step out of the car and open the door for her. I caught a glimpse of her from the side.

Dark hair gathered in a ponytail beneath a blue baseball cap with red lettering and a Puma insignia. She wore designer sunglasses with oversized brown frames and a windbreaker over tights. She was built like a dancer and strutted along with the confidence that her taut physique inspired.

The Macan drove away. I assumed Sarah Dumont was going to work out for at least half an hour, and most likely something between forty-five minutes and two hours. Few classes took less than thirty minutes, and most folks supplemented their organized activity with some sort of personal workout, even if it was comprised solely of abdominal work or stretching. Nevertheless, I waited ten minutes before getting out of the car to make sure the Macan wasn't doubling back.

I tied a scarf around my head and put on my own sunglasses to disguise my appearance. Strange, I thought. Sarah Dumont was the local resident walking around in a baseball cap, a decidedly American style, and I was the American walking around in what I thought was a more European-looking headgear. Perhaps neither one of us was what she seemed.

I opened the door and peaked in the lobby. When I didn't spy her anywhere, I popped inside. A girl behind the front desk was babbling on the phone in Dutch. I grabbed a flier with membership information in English, hid beside a glass fridge filled with energy and protein drinks, and studied the workout facility.

The open gym area contained cardio equipment on one side and resistance equipment on the other. Twenty or so people were exercising, some being put through their paces by personal trainers. Some of the trainers looked the part, while others didn't. That baffled me. How could you inspire others to get fit when you couldn't motivate yourself to do the same? Two rooms with glass walls lined the far wall of the gym. The door to one them whipped open and a man drenched in sweat emerged as a heavy bass from a disco beat groaned behind him. At least thirty cyclists spun their legs madly as a woman in pink tights exhorted them to move. I spotted the ponytail, baseball cap and waifish physique on a bike in the back row.

I ambled back to the front desk, where the girl told me the spin class ended in fifteen minutes. I returned to my taxi, programmed Sarah Dumont's number into my mobile phone, and waited.

The Macan arrived at ten minutes before noon, almost two hours after the driver had dropped her off. Sarah Dumont moseyed out of the gym five minutes later sipping from a straw planted in a pint-sized plastic cup filled with a moss-colored liquid. They drove toward the City Centre and parked on the side of the street beneath a sign that forbid parking.

"Eh?" the taxi driver said. "Only the police or government officials can park there."

Either the private security force consisted of former cops, Sarah Dumont was related to a current politician, or she had real influence for other reasons, I thought.

She got out of the car and headed into town on foot. To my dismay, the driver got out of the Macan and began to follow her.

"Park around here somewhere," I said, flinging the door open. "I'll be back."

"Park where?" my driver said. "All the spaces along the street are taken."

"Adapt, improvise, overcome. Try to stay within the radius of a block. I'll find you."

I could hear him complaining even after I closed the door but I knew he'd be in the vicinity when I returned, just as surely as the cash I owed him was still in my wallet.

Sarah Dumont marched down one of the ubiquitous cobblestone streets. Her driver followed and I stayed twenty paces behind him. The side streets in Bruges were more like glorified alleys. The surrounding buildings blocked all sunlight unless it was shining directly overhead and created the illusion of perpetual twilight. The alleys fed the Burg Square, which appeared as a light at the end of the alley. Sarah Dumont turned left at the light and disappeared. Ten seconds later her driver did the same.

I picked up my pace. As I approached the mouth of the alley, I stopped short of the Burg Square, hugged the left wall, and snuck a peak around the corner.

The driver stood with his back to me five feet away. He was staring into the entrance of some sort of establishment. I pulled my head back, circled to the opposite wall, and took a sharp right out of the alley and into the Square. I stepped into a crowd gazing at the window of the Duman chocolate shop, and used the beer-loving patriarch of a family of four as cover. I turned.

Sarah Dumont stood talking to the driver with a white cardboard carton in her hand. The container overflowed with Belgian fries. I glanced at the establishment from which she'd emerged. It was a fast food joint that claimed to sell the best Belgian frites in Bruges. Based on what I'd seen last night, it was not the only one that made such a claim. She appeared to speak with conviction to the driver, who nodded his head several times, as though understanding her orders. Then he turned, marched back into the alley from which we'd come, and disappeared. Sarah Dumont ate five fries, threw the rest in the garbage, and headed toward a medieval church in the corner of the Square.

I made two immediate observations. First, I could have never stopped myself after only five fries. Second, this was my opportunity.

I took off after her. My mark walked purposefully into the side entrance to the church as though she had an appointment. I was thirty paces behind her so I picked up my pace and pulled the phone out of the inside pocket of my bag. Nothing could slow a person down or send her scurrying out of a church faster than a phone call.

I dialed Sarah Dumont's number. After the first ring, I realized her phone might not be turned on. I immediately discounted that as highly unlikely. She was a successful artist who undoubtedly needed to be plugged into her network at all times. After the second ring, I decided that she might have the phone muted so that she could see if someone familiar was calling her. After the third ring, I entered the church through a narrow door with a curved stone arch.

The ringing stopped. I heard the sound of labored breathing.

"Hello?" I said, keeping my voice down as I stepped inside the vestibule of the church.

I was expecting a woman to answer in kind, with a note of confusion perhaps, given my number would be unknown to her. Instead, a man responded with eerie self-assurance.

"Hello, Ms. Tesla," he said.

I stopped in my tracks.

"Who is this?" I said.

"Turn around."

I whipped my head around.

Sarah Dumont's driver lifted a mobile phone from his ear and waved hello with it. At close range, I recognized him immediately. He was the man who'd held the Uzi that I'd mistaken for the steering wheel locking device. He was power-walking through the entrance to the church toward me. He was only fifteen paces away.

I turned back toward the pews.

The second security guard – the one who'd held the leash on the wolf – was marching straight toward me from the altar. As soon as our eyes met, his hand moved inside his jacket. A smattering of tourists stood admiring the altar, but they were twenty rows in front of the second guard.

The driver was five paces away. The second guard would arrive five seconds later. I remembered the change in De Vroom's manner once he ran the license plate and learned the identity of the Macan's owner. He'd used my Christian name, and warned me with uncharacteristic empathy.

Had I listened?

Of course not.

I could have screamed but for all I knew they had sound suppressed guns tucked in their belts and would kill me anyways. Given my sense of self-preservation, I decided that sticking around to find out was an imprudent choice.

A set of stairs leading below beckoned to my left.

I flew down them. The stairs turned twice. I counted twenty-eight of them before I got to the landing.

Two medieval doors made of petrified wood opened into a church hall. It contained a centuries-old table the length of a yacht and two dozen high chairs with burgundy cushions. I knew from my experience as an altar girl that the priest's vestibule usually featured stairs that led to the basement to allow him private access to and from the altar. Why would churches have been structured any differently in centuries past?

I rushed into the hall and spied doors on both sides of the far wall. A wave of optimism hit me. The doors probably led to staircases. I took aim for the stairway on the right.

An eerie creaking sound behind me was followed by a boom.

I glanced to my rear.

The doors had swung shut. Then I heard a rush of footsteps from the direction where I'd been heading.

I turned again.

The second security guard burst out of one of the doorways. Just as I suspected, there was a staircase in the back, but I'd never considered a man might be racing down its steps to capture or kill me.

I was alone in the bowels of a medieval church with an armed man. I understood De Vroom's warning now. I suspected this was exactly what he feared would happen.

Except we weren't alone.

Sarah Dumont stepped out of the shadows where the doors had stood open. She walked toward me slowly, without saying a word. An unsettling confidence punctuated her movements. She strutted and swung her arms as though she were the big boss in the prison yard. When she got to within three feet of me, she stopped, took off her sunglasses, and then her baseball cap, too.

I recognized her immediately, even without the blond wig.

Sarah Dumont wasn't the mystery lover's mother, aunt, or guardian.

She was the mystery lover.

CHAPTER 10

She stood like royalty, shockingly assured and inscrutable given her youth. Sarah Dumont had the skin of an angel. I had to take a moment to process this because I'd been expecting a boy's mother, not someone younger than me. The taxi driver's story about the home invasion in Amsterdam, her palatial home, and her reported achievements in the theater had reinforced my expectation that she was my elder. But that was clearly not the case.

She spoke with an enviable French accent, the kind that turned English words into hourglass figurines and bestowed upon her an illusion of superior femininity. But she delivered her words with the affectation of an evil godmother in the fairy tale of her own invention.

"Who are you?" she said, tilting her head to the side and studying me as though I were a visitor from a land unknown.

"My name is Nadia Tesla—"

"I know your name. I know what you do. That's not what I asked you. I asked you, who are you?"

"Surely you recognize me," I said.

"Really?" She brought her face so close to mine I could smell the frites on her breath. "I don't think so. I've never seen you before in my entire life. But who knows? I may be wrong. Let me see the rest of you."

She began to circle around me as though I were a sculpture for sale.

I guessed it was possible she really didn't recognize me. She'd only seen me for a second beneath two red light bulbs in the dead of night before running away

"In the window," I said. "In *De Wallen*. On *Ouderkerksplein* ..."

She disappeared from my line of vision, and the knowledge that she'd slipped behind me unnerved me as much as it scared me. I wouldn't have been surprised if she'd grabbed my ass or told her security guard to ensure I never followed her again.

"In *De*-who," she said. "On *Ouder*-what?"

"The woman in the green bikini. The woman who followed you to the Porsche that whisked you away. That was me."

A moment of silence followed, and then I felt her hand brush my shoulder. Her touch imparted a feeling of subordination, reinforced my relative powerlessness, and freaked me out. It also conveyed an unlikely bolt of sexual electricity and turned my attention to the matter that never strayed far from my consciousness. I wondered if this was what my husband had felt when his lover had first laid a hand on him.

"I have no idea what you're talking about," Sarah Dumont said, as she continued circling and returned to my line of sight.

"In Amsterdam. Saturday night. At the anointed time. At midnight."

"I haven't been to Amsterdam in eighteen months. It's not a place I visit anymore."

"I'm here for Iskra," I said. "By now you must have made an inquiry. You must know that she was murdered."

Sarah Dumont faced me. She put her hands on her hips and straightened her lips, and if claps of thunder had erupted outside the church I wouldn't have been surprised.

"You told my security that you wanted to speak to me about my son," she said. "I have no children, I don't know any Iskra, and I don't like strangers coming to my home or following me around town. Now, I have one final question for you. Do you want to leave me alone, or do you want me to show you why you should leave me alone?"

I didn't understand the origins of Sarah Dumont's gall, but it couldn't have been strictly a function of her personality. Someone of power was standing behind her lending credence to her threats, of that I was certain. I was also sure that the most prudent course of action for me was to tell her I was going to leave her alone and get out of town.

"He removed her reproductive organs, you know," I said. "And cut her breasts off. This was after he crucified her to a wall in her apartment."

Sarah Dumont stared at me. As the seconds passed, her expression gradually turned to one of resentment, as though I'd wronged her by sharing the details of Iskra's plight. She looked away and back at me, each time with more anger. Finally, she exhaled and shrugged.

"The girl was just sex to me but if that's what happened to her, that's just wrong. Come, I'll buy you lunch. You get an hour to ask whatever questions you want but after that, I'm done. And if you ever come snooping around my house again I'll have you killed."

CHAPTER 11

She led me to the back door of one of the countless restaurants along the perimeter of the city centre. A note was taped to a side window.

"Due to the Swedish Barmaid falling off her bike pissed and the boss selling sexual favors in warmer climates, Café Bottoms Up will be closed for the rest of the week."

The note made me smile on the inside.

"No, I'm not the boss," Sarah Dumont said, with a note of disgust. "I'm the boss's boss, if that's what you were thinking."

"Not at all," I said.

She glared at me.

I shrugged. "I never thought for a second that you were the Swedish barmaid."

"I hope not. I'm sure there's some food in the refrigerator but I can't cook."

"I can."

She cast a look of surprise at me. "Really?"

Five minutes later I was cooking a large omelet in a copper skillet atop a state-of-the-art range in a gleaming stainless-steel kitchen. While I prepared the eggs, she opened a bottle of chardonnay and warmed some day-old bread in the oven. I split the omelet in half and served the eggs on some smashing Villeroy and Bach plates with a farmhouse design. We sat down to eat in a cozy dining room with country French furnishings and contemporary impressionist paintings on the walls.

"How are my eggs?" I said. "Not quite as fluffy as you're used to, I bet."

Her hesitation confirmed I was correct. "They're good," she said. She looked down at her food. "How did she die?"

"The way I told you," I said. "The way no human being deserves to die."

"No. That's not enough. I want to know exactly how she died."

"Respectfully, I'm not sure there's any benefit to that."

She stared at me with the unblinking eyes of a woman used to giving orders and having them followed. Once again this surprised me because she was so young.

"Let me be the judge of what's beneficial to me, yes?" she said.

I told her everything. Her reaction was in sharp contrast to the tear-stained and traumatized carriage of Iskra Romanova's father. She was quietly respectful but showed no signs of grief.

"When you saw me in *De Wallen* on Saturday night," I said. "You came because you thought Iskra was still alive, obviously."

"It was just fun for me," she said. "I'd never been with a woman before. The first time we fucked she put her lips on me and sucked me the way you'd suck a peach when you're trying to keep the juices from running all over your mouth. She must have kept it up for … ten or fifteen minutes? I don't know. I'm not sure how long. By the end I was barely conscious. It was this gentle, constant, excruciating suction. The pressure built up inside me … I thought I was going to come so badly I would die. Have you ever felt like that? Have you ever had sex so good you thought you would die from the orgasm?" She reached out and touched my arm. "I'm talking about really dying from it."

I smiled because I didn't know what else to do. I'd had plenty of thoughts of death and orgasms since I'd arrived in Amsterdam and taken on the case. In fact, I still had high hopes for those sea salt caramels at Puccini's.

"That sounds like reason enough to want to know who killed her," I said.

Sarah pursed her lips and nodded as though she'd come to a profound realization. "You know, you're right. I may never have sex that good again in my life. I mean, I'm still young, but you can't take anything for granted." She turned her attention back to her food. "We only saw each other nine times. We always met at her office."

"Why?"

"I'm not sure. It was a game. Or that's how it turned out. We met in Tilburg at a T.R.A.S.H. performance."

"What's that?"

She sighed as though I were an idiot. "T.R.A.S.H. is the cutting edge of dance in Holland. Actually, it's more than dance. It's a combination of dance, performance art, and live music. I'm friends with Kristel, the choreographer. I was in town to see a performance. Iskra was there for an audition for a summer series. Something she could do between semesters at school. Kristel asked me to sit in."

"Did Iskra get the part?"

"No, but she got me. You know how sometimes a man stares at you, and it's not because he admires your brain?"

"Only when I diet, tan and wear a lime green bikini."

"That's funny," Sarah said, giving me another unsettling once-over. "You're one of those insecure types that has a lot more going for her than she wants to admit. That's how Iskra looked at me. Like those men. Like she wanted to consume me. It gave me goosies. It gave me goosies up and down my arms. I wanted her right then and there. That never happened to me before with a woman."

"So you agreed to meet in *De Wallen*?"

She nibbled on some bread and nodded.

"She told you she was a prostitute?"

Sarah Dumont smiled. "No. That was the sexy part. She gave me a business card. No title. Just a name, an address, and a mobile number. She said she worked late, to show up at midnight. I figured she worked out of her home. I thought I was going to her apartment."

"Instead you found her standing in a window with a green bikini and headphones on, sipping mineral water from a bottle."

"Mmm. So sexy."

"Was it just sex or did you talk, too?"

"No talking. Until the last night we were together."

My ears perked up. "What happened then?"

"She asked me if I wanted to get a drink. I said 'sure.' We went to bar and talked for two hours."

"What did you talk about?"

"Her. We sure as hell didn't talk about me."

"Why do you say that?"

Once again Sarah Dumont glanced at me as though I were devoid of brain cells. "Why would I want a sex worker to know anything about my business?"

"So you really had no feelings for her."

"My body had feelings for her body. She gave me pleasure. But a woman with another woman, like in a relationship ... That's not natural and it sure as hell is not for me."

"I'm guessing she felt differently?"

"You guessed right. She'd fallen for me, big time. Don't ask me why. We didn't know anything about each other. Maybe it was because I'm a fast learner, and it didn't take long for me to give as good as I got."

"Did she tell she was in love with you?"

Sarah Dumont rolled her eyes. "Poor thing. It was painful to listen to but I didn't want to upset her so I went along with it."

"You mean her body was still providing your body with pleasure, and you didn't want to lose the opportunity for more of the same."

She raised her fork and pointed it at me. "You're a smart woman, aren't you? Yeah, that's about right."

"What did she tell you about herself?"

"She said she knew she was a lesbian since her early teens but she'd never told her parents. She said they were old-school Russians and they'd never understand. Said her father would have gone nuts if he knew. Disowned her, stopped paying for university."

"She was sure of that?"

"And how. She told me that there's no sympathy for gays and lesbians in Russia. None whatsoever. She said being gay was considered a mental illness in Russia until 1990. That seventy-five percent of Russians think being homosexual is immoral. That you can't work with children in Russia if you're gay. And if you have a job in child care and they find out you're gay, you're fired."

"That doesn't surprise me," I said.

"And if you talk about gay rights in front of a child you can be arrested for espionage. You can be tried for treason and killed. And there's a movement to pass a law that would allow the government to take children away from gay people."

I remembered George Romanov's assertion that homosexuality and pedophilia were somehow connected.

"And Iskra's father is sympathetic to all of this crap," I said.

"You say that as though you met him," Sarah Dumont said.

"I had lunch with him."

"Iskra said Russians think Americans spread the word about homosexuality like a weapon. To destroy the moral fabric of Russian children and ruin their society. I guess the government has brainwashed them. I mean, don't get me wrong. I have plenty of gay friends and I don't think it's moral, but neither is prostitution and I had a real good time with one myself. To each his own, you know?"

"Did Iskra give you a key to her apartment?" I said.

"What for? To tell you the truth, I liked her better when I didn't know anything about her. Once she showed she was just another needy girl. I was automatically turned off. Not that I wouldn't have sampled the goods a few more times ..."

This time I paused for a few seconds and let her finish her food and sip her wine. I didn't want to appear overeager with my final query.

"Are your parents originally from Belgium or the Netherlands?" I said.

Sarah Dumont stared me down. That question didn't have any obvious bearing on Iskra's death. I knew it, and she knew it, too. I'd asked it out of curiosity, because her age and profession didn't seem consistent with her lifestyle. Contrary to what the taxi driver had suggested, I hadn't found much about her on the internet. She'd been the choreographer of two highly acclaimed dance shows and had won accolades across Europe. But I doubted that success could have generated sufficient income to build her glass mansion in Bruges.

"That's okay," she said. "I don't mind you asking. I'm proud of my parents. My mother's Belgian. She's a school teacher here in Bruges. My father started out as a city planner in Brussels. He made a lot of contacts. Then he went into construction. He was very successful. He died three years ago. He left my mother and me very comfortable."

"I'm sorry for your loss," I said. "And you've lived in Bruges long? I saw your house from the gate last night. It's very beautiful."

"You know how long I've lived here. The taxi driver or someone in the hotel would have told you that. Wherever you go, one thing stays the same. People love to know other people's business. I lived in Holland for a while, but that didn't work out for me so I moved out here to be with my mother. I can get to anywhere in Europe pretty quickly. But listen, you're asking the wrong questions."

"What are the right questions?" I said.

"You should be asking me who else had a key to her apartment."

I smiled, and she answered without making me ask the obvious question.

"Sasha had a key," she said.

Sasha was the boy I'd seen in Iskra's photos, the one whom her father had dismissed as an innocent family friend.

"How do you know that?" I said.

"She told me."

"Why?" It seemed incredible that during their first conversation outside the bed, Sasha's name would come up.

"We were talking about the fact she kept her sexuality a secret. That she had to keep it a secret given her parents were hardcore Russians. I asked her if anyone knew and she said yeah, her friends at school knew. She had a lot of guy friends from school. Her father thought they were all boyfriends but they were just beards. Whoever said men were useless never needed to keep her lesbian ways a secret."

Her final comment struck a chord, but I chose to ignore it and stay on point. "So none of Iskra's Russian friends knew she was a lesbian or a prostitute, until . . . "

"Until Sasha followed her to *De Wallen* one night."

"When was this?"

"About a week before she was killed."

"What happened?"

"She came home that night after work and found him waiting for her in her apartment drunk. She said he scared the hell out of her, which was why she told me the story in the first place. He insulted her, called her a dyke and a whore, told her he'd hate her for the rest of her life. Which, of course, was a lie."

"Sasha was in love with Iskra."

"Sounded like it to me," Sarah Dumont said.

"Then what happened?"

"She said she called him the next day and the day after that but he never called back."

I pushed my chair back. I had to return to Amsterdam as soon as possible.

"He's too obvious, right?" Sarah said.

"Excuse me?"

"This Sasha. He can't possibly have killed Iskra. He's too obvious."

"In my experience," I said, "the solutions to most problems are fairly obvious. The challenge is to understand the problem in the first place."

"And what was Iskra's problem?" Sarah Dumont answered her own question. "She had to lead a double life, right? On the one had she was her parents' daughter, but on the other hand she had to be herself."

"No," I said. "That would have been bad enough. She chose to lead a triple life. She was someone's daughter, her own woman, and the girl in the window in *De Wallen*."

"Which one got her killed?"

I stood up to leave. "That's what I have to figure out."

CHAPTER 12

Four hours later I was back in Holland and returning to an historic residential neighborhood which also contained an infamous red-light district. From Amsterdam to Bruges and back, from one murky set of waterways to another, I seemed to be following the canals wherever my investigation led me. Now I was right back where it all started, in *De Wallen*, the place where forbidden dreams came true.

I'd called George Romanov from the train to Brussels and asked him to arrange a meeting with Sasha. "Sasha is Sasha," Romanov had said, when I'd queried him about the boy's relationship with Iskra in her apartment. In fact, Sasha's full name was Sasha Norin, and like so many of his generation, he called himself an entrepreneur.

Romanov told me that Sasha was a graphic artist who was trying to build a clothing empire. He'd started out by making designer t-shirts. His brand was currently featured in a dozen stores in the Amsterdam and Rotterdam areas. Meanwhile, to support himself, he moonlighted as a tour guide at the Hash, Marijuana, and Hemp Museum. Yes, there really was such a place in Amsterdam. It was right around the corner from the Cannabis College.

The Museum's main level was filled with what looked like museum quality prints, books and even a miniature reproduction of a ship. Romanov had told me to look for an awkward-looking young man. What I saw instead was a gangly, Rastafarian-looking man-child with rat's whiskers all over his face. He wore jeans, a yellow t-shirt with a jungle motif, and a monstrous green, gold and red Rasta hat that looked more like a sock for elephants. Gnarly dreadlocks fell from the bottom of the hat. I couldn't tell if they were part of the hat or his own. Given the authenticity of my surroundings, I strongly suspected they might be real.

I waited for him to finish speaking to a family of three. Then I walked over to him.

"Sasha?" I said in Russian.

His face lit up as though he'd been waiting for me all day. "Yeah, mon. You must be Nadia."

He sounded like Bob Marley after a heavy diet of blintzes and borsch, the product of Russian and Jamaican parents, which he was not. That he had answered in English was a bold assertion that his English was better than my Russian. I doubted that was true but it would have been rude for me not to switch languages.

He led me to a painting of several weeds hanging on a wall. I'd never smoked anything in my life. Not a cigar, cigarette, and certainly not marijuana. I understood and respected its medicinal applications. Full-stop. But where recreational use was concerned, even where legal, I couldn't contemplate enjoying it more than a glass or three of some fine wine.

"Did you know that only the mature female species makes you high?" he said.

I thought of Iskra and Sarah Dumont. The only problem with that association was that neither of them seemed very mature.

"If only you could say the same for the human race," I said.

He laughed without hesitation. His easy-going nature surprised me. I'd expected an introverted recluse, bitter, sad and angry that his unrequited love had died. But he channeled no such vibe. What he did channel was congeniality, which boded well for me. He was listening, seemed intelligent, and was willing to speak with me. After George Romanov, Sarah Dumont, and even my client, Simmy Simeonovich, I was grateful for the prospect of having a straightforward conversation with a person of interest.

"Downstairs, in the seed bank store," he said, "we weed out the boring males. So they don't dilute the mature female's potency."

"But if you do that, don't you end up with a bunch of egocentric, unstable males?"

Sasha never stopped smiling. "Yeah, mon, but that's what the mature female seed wants. She uses them for her own benefit. Reproduction is all the male is good for. After she's done with them, no one has any use for them."

"Don't tell them that."

"No worries, Miss Nadia. God created every herb and called them all good. You want to try a sample downstairs before we talk?"

"Never on a weekday for me, thanks."

A group of eight college-aged tourists entered the Museum. I motioned to the far corner of the room. Sasha nodded right away, understanding I wanted privacy. We huddled beside a poster from a 1936 movie titled "Marihuana: The Weed with Roots in Hell!"

"I'm sorry about Iskra," I said. "I know you were both close."

His reaction made it seem as though I'd pulled on his dreadlocks, opened a spout in his head, and all his joy had gushed out. He hung his head, and for a moment, I was afraid the weight of his Rasta hat might tip him over. His reaction to my question reminded me of George Romanov, who'd also fallen apart as soon as I asked about his daughter.

"Mr. Romanov said you were awesome," Sasha said. "That he'd never met a woman as tough as you. He said you were committed. That you were going to find out who killed her. He said you were Russian, too."

A bit of light shone in Sasha's eyes when he accused me of having a similar ancestral heritage, and I was not inclined to dim it even though that's exactly what I wanted to do.

"That's right," I said, my ears in partial disbelief that I was willing to tell this lie. "My parents came from the former Soviet Union." There was no need to mention Ukraine.

"Cool, mon. Given you're an American, you know ... It's not the easiest thing to trust an American these days ... This makes it a lot easier. Tell me what you want to know? I'll tell you anything if it helps you find the killer. Anything at all."

"Iskra's father said you grew up together?"

"We were both born in Russia. My father was a government official. He worked with sportsmen, national teams, that sort of thing. After capitalism came to Russia, my father and Iskra's father went into the sporting goods business. They became the biggest distributors of sports equipment in all of Russia. Then they got bought out and we all moved here when we were kids. My parents died, first my father, then my mother, when I was still a kid. The Romanovs sort of adopted me. I was really lost back then. They saved me."

"So you and Iskra, you were like brother and sister?"

He hesitated for a moment as though considering his answer, then nodded. "Exactly like that." He followed up with some nervous laughter. "We used to fight in our teens, mon. Just like cat and dog, you know? But I never had nothing but love in my heart for that girl, and she knew that, yeah she did."

"Is that why you followed her to De Wallen, got drunk, ambushed her in her apartment, and called her a dyke and a whore?"

That earned me a double take and a stern look, but Sasha quickly reverted to his laid-back self.

"Not my finest moment," he said, "but I apologized the next day." His chin rose. He studied me with suspicious eyes. "How did you know ... I didn't tell anyone about that ..."

I wasn't about to reveal Sarah Dumont as my source.

"Were you shocked when you saw her in the window in a green bikini, selling herself to any man that came by?"

Sasha started to clench his teeth, but then smiled as though suddenly realizing that I was provoking him to see if he would lose his cool and what else he might admit to.

"Wouldn't you have been?" he said.

"Big time," I said. "But not as shocked as I would have been when I realized that one of her clients was a woman. How did you figure that out? You must have followed that one client. Why did you do that?"

"I didn't need to follow her. I bumped into her on the side-walk after she left Iskra's room on purpose. Just to get a close look at her face."

I'd seen Sarah Dumont sans make-up and she'd fooled me.

"And you could tell just by looking at her up close that she was a woman?" I didn't believe him for a minute.

"No, mon," he said, sounding even-keeled, not overly solici-tous or defensive, as though what he was about to say was the gospel truth. "When I bumped into her my hand accidentally touched her between the legs. And there was nothing there, you know? Nothing. That's when I knew."

"So then you got drunk and went into Iskra's apartment and waited for her. Meaning you had a key to her apartment and you could come and go as you pleased, right?"

"No," he said, without hesitation. "It wasn't like that at all. I respected her. I never bothered her. Sometimes I'd call her up and she'd say come over for a beer. She used to drink Grolsch and then when she started drinking that Belgian stuff I knew some-thing was wrong. She gave me the key because she trusted me. She lost her key all the time and always had to call her parents to let her in. And she hated when they came by because her mother would always nose around in all her personal stuff. So she gave the key to someone she could trust to be there for her if she locked herself out. She gave it to me."

I spied moisture in his eyes, not necessarily the kind that grew to tears, but still an honest indication that the topic was causing the speaker genuine distress.

"Did you kill her, Sasha?"

"Me?"

"You were so hurt, so angry, maybe you lost your composure the way we're all prone to do with the ones we love, the ones we care about so much when they've done something that hurts us so much."

Sasha looked dejected, as though I'd made the worst possible accusation. "No," he said firmly.

He brought his hand up to wipe his eyes. I noticed the watch around his wrist for the first time. Evidently my agenda and his Rasta-Russian looks had distracted me from spotting it before. It was a stainless steel Panerai chronograph, noteworthy for its elegance and exclusivity. I recognized it because I'd seen Simmy wearing one when he was dressed casually. I didn't know the price tag, but what was a struggling entrepreneur doing with a watch suitable for an oligarch?

"Nice watch," I said.

He glanced at and pulled his arm to his side, as though I'd discovered something he was supposed to hide.

"Oh. Yeah, thanks. It was my father's. He bought it as a gift to himself after he sold his business in Russia.

"It's nice that you wear it." I cleared my throat. "Do you know anyone who would have wanted to harm Iskra? A jilted boyfriend? A jealous rival from school?" I almost said "other jilted boyfriends" but I caught myself just in time.

"No one like that," he said. "But there was that guy in *De Wallen.* He was obsessed with her. I told the cops about it. I don't know if they checked him out or not. But then, I don't even know if they want to solve the murder or not. I mean, Iskra was Russian, and this is the Netherlands, you know?"

"Who was this man?"

"Her bodyguard. At the window. He had a nickname of some kind." Sasha scrunched his eyes as he tried to remember.

"The Turk?"

Sasha snapped his fingers. "That's it."

"How do you know he was obsessed with Iskra?"

"She told me."

"What? When?"

"That night. When I was in her apartment waiting for her. She blurted out that she was already having problems with a guy at work and she didn't need any more from me. Next day when I called to apologize I pressed her for details because I was worried about her, you know? That's when she told me his name. She made me swear to keep it to myself and never go near him. She said he wouldn't hesitate to hurt me if I upset him."

"She said that to you?"

"She did."

"And you told the police this?"

"I did."

I wrapped things up with Sasha. He gave me his mobile phone number and address without hesitation. I wanted to leave on the most congenial note possible, so I put my hand on his shoulder and thanked him for his help. Some light reappeared in his eyes when he felt my touch and heard my words, and he bid me farewell with a smile.

I'd arrived at the Hash, Marijuana and Hemp Museum mildly intoxicated about what Sasha might reveal about Iskra and its potential benefits to my investigation. I left as sober as the girl who was never asked to dance at the ball. I felt as though I was walking around in circles, literally and figuratively.

On the surface, Sasha's assertion that the Turk had been obsessed with Iskra presented a new suspect with a potentially powerful motive. If he'd fallen in love with her, he might have demanded that she quit the business. Alternatively, he might have been horrified to discover that one of her clients was a woman. That seemed less likely for a man who worked with prostitutes for a living. More likely was a scenario where Iskra admitted to the Turk that a woman had won her heart. Perhaps that had infuriated him past the point of self control.

But was he the calculating type who would plan and stage a despicable act of cruelty? Did I picture the Turk as a meticulous planner who'd bring a stud finder to mount his victim on a wall with a carpenter's precision? No, I did not. He was more likely to snap, which was to say he was more likely to snap her neck in a moment of fury. Still, I couldn't be certain of this.

The only firm conclusion I could come to after my meeting with Sasha was that all leads brought me back to *De Wallen*.

The Turk worked in *De Wallen*. And that is where I would have to return if I wanted to speak with him.

I made a U-turn, picked up my pace and headed back toward Iskra's – and my – office. The red lights were on above the windows of the African girls' offices on *Ouderkerksplein*. I could see their fleshy outlines in the windows closest to mine. It was still early by the red-light district's standard, and there were only a few passersby when I arrived. My office was dark and empty as expected.

I unlocked the door, stepped inside, turned on the interior light, and took a deep breath.

Then I hit the panic button, stepped back outside, and waited.

CHAPTER 13

Footsteps pounded toward me. They came from inside the apartment building, just as they had when the Turk first appeared in my office after the landlady pressed the panic button as a demonstration. I turned from my doorway and saw someone entering my office through the inner door.

He was the Turk's young protégé.

Someone slammed me from behind.

I stumbled, teetered, took aim for the bed and landed face first on the mattress. The sheet smelled deliciously crisp and clean with a faint scent of a floral garden. The outside door closed behind me. I knew I'd just become a prisoner in my own office and yet here I was, marveling at the diligence of the window prostitutes' cleaning service. The things I noticed at the most unlikely times never ceased to amaze me. I wondered if the wiring in my brain was off.

As I rose to my feet, I heard a deep voice bark instructions from behind. The protégé scampered out of the room and closed the door behind him. I recognized the Turk's voice. I knew it was he who'd given the orders even before I turned around.

The sight of the Turk jarred me nonetheless. It wasn't his rawboned structure or the gargantuan size of his head, but rather his constantly seething nature. Menace oozed from his pores and left one wondering how many miles his engine could log before it expired.

He locked the door from the inside and stood with his back to it. In the event I needed to leave immediately, I would never get past him. The only escape was through the interior door, and that assumed it wasn't locked.

The Turk opened his hip-length leather jacket and started to undo his belt.

"What are you doing?" I said.

"Preparing to get paid."

"What?"

"Preparing to get paid," he said. "You came back here. You're not really a professional. You dressed up like the dead girl so you were probably working for her family, trying to find her killer. Am I right?"

He was right, of course, but I didn't admit that to him. I was too shocked by the realization that I'd underestimated him so badly.

"Surprise, surprise, American woman. The Turk is not as stupid as he looks."

He dropped his pants, stepped out of them and tossed them onto the bed. I tried not to glance at his mostly bare lower body but my eyes went there of their own accord. Hair on top of hair on surprisingly spindly legs, black leather underwear in the finest Speedo tradition, and of course, the requisite bulge that he probably thought was a major turn-on. I suppressed a surge of bile, and finally, a surge of adrenaline told me I'd better do something fast.

I made the time-out sign. "Whoa, my strong and handsome friend. Stop right there." I picked up his pants and tossed them back at him. "Put those back on."

He crossed his arms over his chest and let the pants fall to the floor. "I will answer your questions only if you pay me."

I tapped my bag, which miraculously still hung off my shoulder by a strap. "Of course I'll pay you."

"Not that way." He grabbed his crotch. "You must pay me the way a woman who rents this room should know how to pay."

"But I'm not that woman. You said so yourself."

"That's not what I said. I said you're not really a professional. But you did rent the office. So you should act like a professional. You should pay me like a professional."

"You want me to act like a professional?" I said. "Okay. I'll act like a professional."

The Turk smiled and nodded.

"I understand that Amsterdam is very protective of its prostitutes," I said. "That the local government has instituted anti-discrimination laws for the protection of legal sex workers. For instance, if a sex worker were to be denied a loan at a bank, and that bank were found to have discriminated against her profession, it could be found guilty in a Netherlands court of law. At this moment, I'm a legally employed sex-worker. You understand that, right?"

The Turk's eyes narrowed, as though he agreed but didn't like the direction in which I was headed, or the confidence with which I was navigating my path.

"What if I filed a complaint? There must be a way I can file a formal complaint against a man who's supposed to be protecting me, the legal sex worker, but instead has tried to force himself upon me twice?"

"That is a lie." The Turk raised his finger and pointed it at me. "I have never tried to force myself on you. I have never touched you."

"I beg to differ. I think it was you who just pushed me in here and locked the door behind him. It will be my word against yours.

I can get a billionaire and a dozen CEOs to swear in court my word is bond. How about you?"

He paused to process what I'd just said.

"Put your pants on," I said, "and let's do some business."

He seethed for a moment, long enough for me to pray the interior door wasn't locked if I needed to run.

"What business?" he finally said.

"You're not as slow as I thought but you're far from Formula One material. I ask, you answer, I pay cash. That kind of business. Good enough?"

He gathered his pants around his waist. I took the sound of his zipper moving northward to be a response in the affirmative.

"Tell me about your relationship with Iskra," I said.

"Relationship?" He shrugged. "What relationship? She worked. I protected. Sometimes I sampled the merchandise. At first I paid, but after a while, she got a taste for the Turk, and I didn't have to pay."

I cast a skeptical look at him. "In case I didn't state the obvious, you lie, you don't get paid. So let's start over. Sometimes you tasted the merchandise. Meaning you paid her for sex?"

"No. I asked her to read the lines on my hand and tell me my future."

"Why did you stop paying her for sex? What do you mean she got a taste for the Turk?"

"She got a taste for the Turk means she got a taste of this." He tapped his heart.

"What is that supposed to mean? That you didn't fall in love with her, but she fell in love with you? Are you kidding me?"

He scoffed. "Love? Love is for the very rich and the very poor, for those who are bored because they have a lot of money, and those with no hope because they have no money." He thumped his fist against his chest again, like a Catholic begging forgiveness for his sins. "Iskra got a taste of what it was like to be with a real man. Not in bed. In life. I protected her. I took care of her. And I didn't judge her. I didn't ask her for anything that she didn't want to do for money. And so ..." He nodded as though his implication were clear.

I was starting to wonder if I was missing something obvious. "Yes? And so?"

"And so she hired me."

His answer took my breath away. That was not a proposition I'd even contemplated.

"Hired you to do what?" I said.

"To protect her."

"From what?"

"Not what," he said. "Who."

"She was scared of someone?"

"Not scared. Terrified."

"Did she tell you who?"

"No."

"She didn't mention a young man?" I said. "A young man named Sasha?"

"She did not name names."

"And what kind of protection did you provide, exactly?"

"I walked her home after work. She said she was no longer comfortable being out at night alone."

"And you did this for her in exchange for sex?"

The Turk nodded. "Twelve times." He shook his head, a longing etched in his face. "That girl was unbelievable. She didn't have sex with you. She *was* sex. She had that gift. You touched her and she melted. There was no acting in her. The first time she put her mouth—"

"Stop," I said. "I've heard the soundtrack to a similar movie before. How do you know she was terrified?"

The Turk bristled. "How did I know? She would walk beside me holding my hand like a scared little kitten. When we got to her apartment, she'd ask me to go in first and check every room to make sure no one was waiting for her."

I pictured Sasha unleashing his full verbal fury after a decade of unrequited love. Was that enough to propel Iskra into a state of perpetual fear? I didn't think so. "Sasha is Sasha," her father had said. That implied there had always been a certain immaturity to him, one that Iskra had undoubtedly seen and managed. Based on the Rosta-Russian man-boy I'd met, I didn't see him inspiring fear any more than I saw him bringing a stud-finder to a meticulously planned crucifixion of the girl he'd loved his entire life.

"Did she ever ask for your help outside of work?" I said.

The Turk shook his head. "I walked her home after she turned off her lights. That's it. Nothing else. If she had asked for more help, I would have given it to her. But she never did."

"When did this all start? When was the first night she asked you to walk her home?"

"Two weeks before she died."

That jibed with the general time frame of when Sasha had discovered Iskra was moonlighting as a sex worker and seeing a woman.

"Did you know that one of her clients was a woman?"

"Of course I knew. I know everything that happens in the rooms that belong to the women I protect."

"Did Iskra ever talk about that woman?"

"Never. And I didn't ask her, either. That would have been against my professional code of conduct. The relationship between a woman and her client is a sacred thing. *It's business.*"

On that note, I opened my wallet and gave the Turk a hundred euro. Given we'd talked for less than fifteen minutes, it was an overly generous hourly rate. He didn't complain or haggle one bit. Instead, he slid the bills gently into his wallet, walked over to the door leading to the streets, and opened it.

"Was I right about why you're here?" he said.

I looked him in the eye but didn't say a word.

He nodded with approval.

"One other thing," I said. "Did she give you a key to her apartment?"

The Turk dismissed the idea with an immediate frown. "Why would she give me a key? We were not friends."

In fact, it didn't matter if she'd given him a key or not. The knew each other. Theoretically, he could have entered her apartment by knocking on the door. But I wanted to see the look on his face when I asked the question. He was clearly more intelligent than I'd assumed and he would have surely realized why I was asking. But he didn't appear concerned that I might consider him a suspect at all.

I walked back to my hotel frustrated yet energized. Sasha had told me that Iskra had said that the Turk was obsessed with her. That was a lie, but I couldn't be certain if it was Sasha or Iskra had fabricated a story. My money was on Iskra. I suspected that one of her clients really was obsessed with her but that she didn't want Sasha confronting him. By lying, Iskra was protecting her childhood friend from someone she considered powerful and dangerous.

She had been scared, mortally so. She'd been afraid to return to her home alone at night. Surely the person whom she was afraid of was this person who was obsessed with her, the one who eventually killed her.

I had an eerie feeling that I was close to the killer and that the most significant piece of information was already in my possession. This suspicion was based on an intuition similar to the one I'd experienced during dozens of corporate investigations. I'd seen all the necessary data points. I simply hadn't visualized them in the proper order yet, which was to say I hadn't spotted the definitive lie among them.

Food was on my mind when I stepped into the hotel lobby. A woman at the front desk called me by name before I could get by.

"There's a gentleman waiting to see you," she said, with a big smile.

Alarm bells sounded in my head. It could only be De Vroom, I thought. He must have found out I hadn't followed his orders and was still looking into Iskra's death.

"Where is this gentleman?" I said.

Two other female hotel employees appeared out of nowhere and stood eyeing me and beaming beside her. I felt like the winner of a pageant I'd never entered.

"In the bar," she said, and motioned toward the glass stairs to my right.

I passed a reading room and entered the restaurant on the left side of a corridor. The bar was positioned on the opposite side of the dining room, behind the kitchen. I took a deep breath and entered the lounge. I expected to see De Vroom sitting on a stool nursing a whiskey, looking like the model in a photo shoot for some beverage aficionado's magazine.

Instead I found Simmy Simeonovich sitting at a table for two. An outrageous bouquet of tulips rested on one side of the small circular table in front of him. Beside it stood a tantalizing box wrapped in glossy red and white paper with a matching bow. He rose to his feet as soon as he saw me, and the cumulative effect of his appearance and the loot on the table was to render me speechless.

"Good evening, Nadia."

He delivered his greeting with a gentle enunciation and a slight bow, like the man I thought I'd befriended two years ago, not like the oligarch who'd chastised me when I'd been released from jail.

"What's in the box?" I said.

"The box?" He glanced at the table. "Oh, that. Forget about that. That's for later."

I was intrigued but reluctant to let him know how happy I was to see him, especially bearing gifts. Hence, I ignored the tulips and put my hand on my hip.

"Why are you here, Simmy?"

"To make amends," he said.

"Excuse me?"

"To make amends. To try to explain to you why I am the man I am and ..." He pursed his lips as though asking me to save him from the embarrassment of having to display any more humility.

"And?" I said.

Even the Simmy I'd known prior to Amsterdam would have bristled at my refusal to cut him any slack. This, however, was not the Simmy I knew. This was someone entirely different.

He straightened his posture and arched his chin a bit. Cleared his throat like a man intent on making sure his words sounded real, true, and hit their mark.

"And I'm here to apologize for my poor behavior, and to ask you to please forgive me." He reached down, wrapped his hand around the bouquet and handed it to me.

I took the flowers from him the way a robot would wash a windshield, mechanically, without any awareness of what I was doing. I knew my ears had not deceived me and that I had heard him correctly, but I didn't believe a word of it. How could I? No man had ever spoken to me in such a heartfelt fashion, let alone one who'd made his vast fortune by eschewing humility and lived in a world where it was considered a weakness.

"Will you have dinner with me?" he said. "Here? Tonight?"

I nodded.

"Excellent," he said.

"I need to go upstairs and freshen up. Did you . . . did you want to come up and wait in my room?"

He smiled and bowed again. "Thank you, but no. It would be more appropriate if I wait for you here."

"Suit yourself," I said.

I turned to leave but decided he deserved a reward for all that he'd said and done so far. I knew how to reward him because I knew it was my irreverent American ways that he enjoyed so much.

"Can I ask you a question before I go?" I said.

"Yes?"

I donned my finest straight-man look and paused a beat for effect. Then I twisted an expression of great curiosity onto my face.

"What's in the box?" I said.

Simmy smiled. "Knowledge."

CHAPTER 14

The restaurant at the hotel was called 5&33 Flavors and it drew inspiration from a traditional Italian tasting plate. Simmy brought his fresh attitude, the mysterious box, and infinite possibilities to the table. I offered gamesmanship, wit, and a challenge for the man who had everything.

But that wasn't enough. No man had ever approached me to make amends over behavior he regretted. No co-workers or bosses, not my brother, deceased father or husband. No, I thought. I would do more than be my finest self. I would try something novel this evening. I would try to channel grace and forgiveness, if he really meant what he said.

My assessment of the prospects for the evening prompted me to make the obvious observation after we sat down at our table and received our menus from our waiter.

"Where are your bodyguards?" I said.

"Where they're supposed to be," Simmy said, without taking his eyes off the menu. "Where they can see you but you cannot see them."

I scanned the dining room. Twenty tables filled a narrow rectangular space. Solitary men occupied three of the tables. Waitresses with golden hair and tossed-back shoulders chatted up two of them. Various couples occupied six of the other tables. None of them resembled Simmy's protectors. A rectangular fire pit provided a barrier between the dining room and a separate lounge area. I spied the bodyguards' reflection in the stainless steel structure that housed the fire and savored the moment.

Perhaps Simmy was right. Maybe I was in possession of some kind of investigative arsenal.

"You're right," I said. "I can't see them."

"Of course you can't. That's why they're my bodyguards."

I knew he liked to study the menu and then ask me to order for him. But he also liked to peruse the wine list with an expert's eye, and that selection he would make himself after I chose his entree. He liked to do this in silence, I knew, because the wine was the most important part of dinner for him, providing him far more pleasure than the food. I never intruded on his study of the wine list with small talk. I sensed that he appreciated my comfort with silence, and that it had been a key element of our instant chemistry.

As soon as I knew what I was going to order for both of us, I set the menu aside to signal I was done. Simmy caught the waiter's attention and motioned for him to come over. We'd followed this routine during our prior dinners, but it wasn't until this evening that I realized how much I enjoyed this private dance. We are often unaware of our most sublime pleasures until faced with the prospect of their extinction.

"The gentleman will start with the goat cheese ravioli with aubergine, pinenuts and basil," I said to the waiter. "I'll have the endive and beetroot salad – no parmesan, please. And we'll have the grilled sea bass for entrees, the one that's for two to share."

Simmy ordered a fabulous-sounding French Chablis and the waiter left.

"Frankly," Simmy said, "I'm disappointed."

I shook my head slowly in an exaggerated fashion. "I don't think so."

He chuckled. "I love it. There is only one Nadia, isn't there? I think I'm disappointed, but you know better."

"Of course I know better. That's why you have me order in the first place."

"Please explain."

"You think you're disappointed because I picked a fish that goes best with a light white wine. By selecting sea bass, I ruled out the chewy reds you love, and the juicy whites you crave, the Montrachets and Meursaults. Am I right?"

He lifted his hand from his chin and twisted it open, palm-up. *Obviously*, he was saying.

"But by foregoing the nectar of the gods, you're practicing delayed gratification. Like me – I wanted the tagliolini with truffles but I won't splurge until I solve this murder – you get to enjoy a nice meal but look forward to something even more special some day soon."

"Something even more special. That's interesting." Simmy lifted his eyebrows. "And we are both practicing this . . . what was it you called it?"

"Delayed gratification."

"That's a new concept to me. Russians are avid practitioners of instant gratification. In fact, it's a national obsession. And since we're both practicing this delayed gratification, we would enjoy this ... this grand feast together, am I right?"

"Theoretically," I said. "I suppose it depends on what happens between now and then."

Simmy cleared his throat, placed his hands on the table and sat up straight. I reached for my water to hydrate and appear nonchalant. Simmy typically carried himself in a relaxed manner that was carefully cultivated to belie his true intensity. Now he looked stiff, formal and awkward, as though he had something serious to say.

Even the water couldn't wash away the bitter-sweet anticipation on the tip of my tongue.

"Then in the spirit of turning the theoretically into the actual," he said, "let me get down to the business at hand."

As I wondered what he was talking about, the extravagantly wrapped box of knowledge caught my eye on the ledge behind him.

"What exactly is the business at hand?" I said.

"Making amends."

"Excuse me?"

"Me ... I ..." He struggled to find the right words. "I must make amends to you for my poor behavior."

I sat there mute for longer than I should have. It was one of those moments comparable to finding a long-lost treasure in a long-forgotten hiding place based on sudden inspiration. It's almost always a figment of one's imagination. But this – this was really happening.

"You weren't kidding," I said.

"No, I most definitely was not. I shouldn't have criticized you for pretending to be a window prostitute. I should have praised you for your ingenuity. I should have insisted you were fed that night I picked you up in jail. I should have told you from the start that my men were watching Iskra Romanova's office and made you aware that this meant that they might end up watching you, too. Above all else, I should have put your good health and comfort above my own. I didn't, and for that I humbly apologize."

I started to form a witty response. That was to be expected because repartee was the magnet that drew us toward each other. But then I remembered my pledge to be graceful and forgiving. Simmy was trying like no man had tried before. He deserved some respect and compassion. He deserved the sentiments I barely knew how to express.

"You're my client," I said, "and you never need to apologize. But given the spirit of what you say, apology accepted."

He took a breath, not too deep but audible enough for me to know my words meant a lot to him.

I considered changing the subject to save us both any further embarrassment. But that would have been weak, I decided. That would have been my strategy with my deceased husband, to always defer, to look for a way to appease his ego. Simmy had apologized. He had humbled himself. This was my opportunity to shine a flashlight into his eyes and see into his soul.

I spoke as gently as I could, which was to say, I chose the flashlight with the dimmest possible light, albeit one whose brightness I could crank up on demand.

"This was ... this is not something I would have ever expected, Simmy. I'm just curious. If you don't mind my asking ... What brought this on?"

"Not what," he said. "Who."

I waited for him to answer his own question.

He did so, but only after looking around to make sure no one was listening. Still, he whispered the answer. "My therapist."

I pulled my head back.

"Actually, my acupuncturist. A young man from China, but he's so spiritually evolved he might as well be my therapist." He shrugged. "A man either evolves or falls victim to his afflictions. I choose the former."

"I couldn't be more impressed," I said, hoping I sounded sincere. "I had a boss who once said that seventy-percent of all businessmen in New York City were taking some sort of medication. And the ones who weren't taking it were fools."

"It's the same in Russia, except the medication is called vodka and its use isn't limited to businessmen."

"When bribery is a way of life," I said, "any person could be driven to drink."

I regretted the words as soon as they rolled off my lips. Not that I didn't mean what I said – I just wished I'd managed to restrain myself and allow the feel-good to last a little longer. But that was probably unrealistic, I realized. Our moment of shared introspection was just that – a moment. A return to the verbal combat that defined us was inevitable.

"I know you think all Russian businessmen are gangsters," Simmy said, "but that is not the case. You can thank your free press and precious Hollywood for that misconception. I am a corporate raider. I bought my companies fair and square."

There was truth in everything he said. After serving his mandatory stint in the army, Simmy had earned his PhD in quantum physics at age twenty-five. He then traded metals on the Russian market to earn enough money to buy his first smelter. He slept near the factory furnace for the first six months to prevent thieves from ransacking his sole asset. He turned a profit, expanded into other commodities, diversified into industrials, and formed the Orel Group, his own conglomerate. At last count the Orel Group owned fifteen companies. Of those, two were Western European and eleven were American. All of them traded on public exchanges.

"You're putting words in my mouth," I said. "I never implied you were a gangster. I just think there's a criminal aspect to how business is conducted in Russia because bribes are commonplace and accepted. It's hard to get the electricity to work without them, right?"

Simmy looked away and shrugged, as though acknowledging a truth of which he wasn't proud. "Thirty years ago we were a communist country. We're not going to fix our thing overnight. It's going to take time. Just like me. It's going to take me time to change."

Once again Simmy's words stunned me. Change came easily for billionaires, but usually in the form of increasingly extravagant living.

"What exactly do you want to change about yourself?" I said. "Granted, I thought you may have been a bit harsh in your car when I got out of jail, but it's not like you're an unrepentant killer ..." I laughed to try to make a joke of my words. "Are you?"

My voice trailed off as I blurted out my question. I meant it figuratively, not literally, but given I was investigating a murder it certainly didn't sound that way when the words left my mouth.

Simmy, however, seemed to understand exactly what I meant.

"In business I must eliminate my competition sometimes," he said. "There is simply no other way. I mean that in a corporate sense, of course. But that doesn't excuse my behavior in my personal life. I've been avoiding my ex-wife, treating her rudely. That is unacceptable because we share custody of two children. I'm not spending enough time with them, either. That's what money does to a man."

"What's that?"

"It makes him want more money. Soon nothing else matters. He begins to forgive himself for his transgressions too easily." Simmy leaned in toward me. His words sounded urgent, his voice almost pleading for me to listen carefully. "What you must understand, Nadia, is that men have no role models in Russia."

Simmy's assertion resonated with me. My deceased husband's parents and my own mother and father had been World War II refugees. They'd trusted no one and seemed incapable of unconditional love. Were their children any better? One Friday morning I took the train from New York City to New Haven and surprised my husband at Yale. When I saw his petite graduate assistant exiting his apartment as I arrived, I confronted him. He backhanded me across the face, insisted he'd never touched another woman, and told me never to question his fidelity again. I took it and did nothing, that time and many times later, as my mother had done before me. I'd always held my husband and myself – not our parents – accountable for our own behavior, but there was truth in what Simmy was saying.

"Russian men don't know how to be husbands or fathers," Simmy said. "Who was there to teach us? The Soviet Union destroyed the Russian family. There was no freedom of speech, religion, or mobility. A man couldn't leave town to see his relatives without permission. The KGB were everywhere. It was an empire built on fear, where men were rewarded for persecuting their neighbors. Ambition served only those connected with the central government. For all others, there was no hope for anything other than to survive. During the twentieth century, the soul of all Russian men was systematically destroyed to preserve the powers of the central government and to let the ruling elite have their way. What kind of husbands and fathers do you think this bred?"

I thought of the Western stereotype of a Russian man, lawless and drunk. "The kind who suffered and medicated his pain any way he could."

"Why does the West think Russian men have a problem with alcoholism? Why do so many Russian marriages end in divorce? Our parents, and their parents, and their parents before them . . . none of them were role models, and none of them are to blame. The life expectancy of a Russian man in 2000 was fifty-eight years. When you go to Russia, you're expected to drink in excess in all social situations. If you don't, Russians view you as a weak person. Why is that?"

I shook my head.

"Because it means you give a shit about your future. Because it means you're actually arrogant enough to think there's hope for you, that you're different than the masses, that you're better than them, that you'll live longer. And so the moment you refuse to drink with your host, your client, your potential business partner, he views you suspiciously. He believes you are someone he cannot trust. And he sure as hell resents you."

I'd only seen Simmy look anxious on one other occasion, when our lives were at risk in a Siberian castle that had belonged to the FBI's most wanted man, Russia's most notorious organized crime leader. But here he was, flashing creases in his temple in the comfort of an Amsterdam restaurant and under the protection of his bodyguards. My observations unnerved me a bit, as to be in Simmy's presence was to feel, above all else, temporarily invulnerable.

"Last time I saw you," I said, "you talked about the European and American sanctions against Russia ... did something else happen?"

Simmy looked around before speaking yet again, and then lowered his voice so low that I had to lean forward and strain to hear him. "Remember my friend – now my former friend – the one who complained about the President to the press? The one that said Valery was to blame for the sanctions and the miserable state of Russian society? He had his wings clipped yesterday."

"A Russian oligarch had his wings clipped? What does that mean?"

"He was the largest printer and distributor of textbooks to primary schools in Russia. Actually, he pretty much had a monopoly. Now, as of yesterday, all schools have stopped ordering books from his company."

"Why?" I said.

"Because his texts have been declared outdated by the central government. As of the next school year, new texts will be distributed by someone else, a company that specializes in appliance repair manuals. And my friend's company is under investigation for illegal business practices."

"What kind of illegal business practices?"

"Bribing government officials," Simmy said.

"Of course. I should have guessed. Did your friend make it out of the country?"

"No. They arrested him four hours ago. The press were there when they took him away – they were stalking him since he complained about Valery so of course they were – and he did something ... he said something ..." Simmy shook his head gravely.

"What?" I said. "What did he say?"

"He said the country needed a change in leadership. He said it was time for a man of integrity to take over the country. A man like Simeon Simeonovich."

I remembered what Simmy had told me about oligarchs getting involved in politics in Russia – it was suicidal.

"You have no interest in politics," I said. "And your friend knew the mere suggestion that you're interested could cast a shadow over you or worse – but he said it anyways ... which is why you just referred to him as your 'former friend.' And his motive for doing this to you was?"

"He asked me to intercede with Valery on his behalf, to apologize and tell him his emotions got the better of him. He thinks Valery and I are such close friends, like father and son, as the press likes to say. But the truth is, we don't have those kind of friendships in Russia. And if I had stepped up for him ..."

"Putler would have become suspicious that you share your friends convictions ..."

"Which he almost certainly thinks now," Simmy said.

I wanted to do something to cheer Simmy up or at least distract him, so I segued into the case and told him about everything that had transpired since I'd last seen him. He was, after all, my client, and I needed him to arrange a meeting with Iskra's mother. She and I had spoken only briefly when I'd first arrived in Amsterdam because she'd been out of town the night Iskra was killed. But I considered her an invaluable source of background information regarding Iskra, her friends, and her lovers.

Simmy called her from the table and arranged for us to meet at breakfast. Then we enjoyed a scrumptious dinner. We talked about his soccer team, his gigayacht, and my business. The one thing we didn't discuss was the deliciously wrapped box. The longer the evening went, the more its contents intrigued me.

After he paid the bill, we walked to the hotel entrance. One of his bodyguards went ahead to retrieve his car, while the other one remained ten paces behind us. Simmy thanked me for my company, and I told him it had been a lovely evening. Then he handed me the box.

"This is for you," he said, "to help you understand the mind of a Russian man."

I took the box in my hands. It felt surprisingly light, no heavier than a roll of paper towels.

He bowed and started toward the circular door.

"This is very mischievous, Simmy. That's all you're going to tell me?"

He glanced back at me. "All will be clear when you open the package."

Simmy left. I took the elevator to the second floor and walked into my room. I wanted to take a shower, and the thought of delaying the opening of Simmy's present carried great appeal. I could lie on the bed in a crisp terry robe with the TV on and order a cup of tea from room service. Some gratification, however, simply could not be delayed.

I tore off the wrapping paper to expose a brown cardboard box. Inside the box was a wooden figurine in the shape of an enormous salt shaker. A girl's face was painted on one side. She had a golden bun for hair, pink balloons for cheeks, triangular blue eyes with black lashes, and silly pink lips the size of a child's kiss. Beneath the face was a colorful bouquet, an impressionist's rendering of pink, burgundy, green and yellow flowers. The figurine's dome was painted steel-blue, the bottom crimson.

I'd grown up with Ukrainian objects of beauty in the house. The *matryoshka*, the nesting doll, was a distinctly Russian creation. I'd heard of them and seen pictures, but I'd never actually held one or played with it. In this instance, I was less interested in the doll, and more curious to see if Simmy had inserted something inside.

The doll came apart in the middle. A twist of the wrist removed the top half and revealed a similar doll inside. My hands trembled as I continued to pull one doll out of another. The sixth doll was half the size of my thumb. I picked it up in my hand and shook it. Something bounced around its interior walls. I pictured Simmy substituting bauble in place of the final doll. Not that gifts or material things mattered much to me. No, they didn't, I reminded myself. Not at all.

I held my breath, removed the cover from the sixth doll, and pulled out the contents from within.

It was a seventh doll. This one, however, was painted yellow, and its face didn't belong to the girl depicted on the other dolls. This face belonged to a little boy.

A pang of disappointment hit me, though I never would have admitted it to anyone. I studied all the dolls again. They had no false bottoms or tops, they contained nothing else inside, and the last doll didn't open at all. All the dolls seemed to weigh proportionately less than the one that had contained it. The smallest doll, the yellow one, didn't unscrew. It felt as though it was made out of air.

It was certainly an object of beauty and a lovely gift. The largest doll's bottom contained a signature and a date. No doubt it was a collectible. But that wasn't why Simmy had given it to me. He'd told me that the doll contained knowledge that would help me understand the mind of a Russian man.

The obvious implication was that a Russian man was a complex amalgamation of multiple personas, at the core of which was a child. If I wanted to understand him, I had to understand each one of his personas. Perhaps one doll reflected how he acted in matters of business, another how he behaved with his children, a third how he made love to a woman. Such a conclusion seemed simple enough.

Simmy was obviously playing a game with me. He'd just challenged me to discover something about him by studying a doll, and that was fine with me.

I was always up for a new challenge.

CHAPTER 15

Iskra's mother looked more like someone in need of salvation and less like a colonel in the army. Granted, just because the Salvation Army used a military hierarchy didn't mean its officers were supposed to look like George Patton or Joan of Arc. Still, I was stunned when Maria Romanova opened the door to greet me at her palatial home by the ubiquitous Amsterdam canal. She welcomed me with a smile but her eyes looked vacant, like the view of a long stretch of desert through a pair of binoculars. Her sweater hung so loosely on her frame I feared she'd misplaced her shoulders. Iskra had been murdered less than two weeks ago, but her mother looked as though she'd been struggling with life for far longer.

I wondered why.

The Romanovs' home was decorated in an opulent French style. The living room reminded me of the most beautiful salons in New York City hotels where I'd attended more than one corporate presentation through the years. Elegant gilding surrounded pistachio-colored boisere. Antique furnishings enhanced the sensation that one had just entered a wealthy Parisian home. Some people might have scoffed at the extravagance of it all, but there was no doubt that the room had been meticulously appointed with impeccable taste.

It was a room built for splendor and joy but even the paneled walls were crying. The musical selection didn't help, some sort of Russian opera with constant wailing from a heavyweight soprano bent on global depression. It was the sort of selection my Ukrainian mother would have made. There was something genetic in Eastern European blood that made its people wallow in mourning. *Why limit your sadness to that which came naturally when you could make yourself truly miserable and reduce your own life expectancy?*

Perhaps that was an unfair assessment and Maria Romanova's selection of music was a virtue. If mourning was the prerequisite to emotional healing, perhaps the pursuit of maximum distress was a shortcut to a return to normalcy. Whatever the truth, there was no doubt that Iskra's mother had loved her daughter. The same could be said for her father, George, I thought, remembering his despair at the murder scene. In fact, I wouldn't have been surprised if the musical selection was a mutual one.

Maria served us tea and croissants. I poured some milk into my tea and added a packet of natural sugar substitute. When I lifted my cup, a plume of steam twisted into the air. As I gazed at my host through the cloud of moisture, she looked like a ghost who'd been summoned at a séance.

"Is George at home?" I said.

I used his first name on purpose to suggest we'd become friends. That wasn't too much of an exaggeration. In her husband's mind, the Russian whore from the decrepit States was his mate for life.

Maria ignored my question as though I hadn't said a word. Instead, she lifted a croissant from the basket with a pair of tongs and dropped it onto her plate. The odd thing was that she dropped it from a foot above its target, and smiled like a child when it landed unscathed.

"George?" Maria said, without looking at me. "He has his morning routine. The gymnasium and then the sauna. Always the sauna. He's one of those Russians that still thinks dehydrating yourself will make you live longer."

"If that's the only way he's dehydrating himself, then it's not the worst thing."

She looked at me as though I'd spoken Japanese. All traces of emotion vanished from her face. It was as though she'd pushed her own personal panic button and her brain had erased her short-term memory. The vacuous look returned to her eyes.

"Who are you again, dear?" she said.

Her question rattled me. I'd just arrived ten minutes ago. She'd been prepared for my arrival and had recognized my name right away.

"I'm Simeon Simeonovich's friend," I said.

Nothing.

"I'm Simmy's friend. I'm the investigator he hired." I stopped short of saying what I was investigating, for fear she might have forgotten her daughter had been murdered.

A spark ignited in her eyes. "Simmy," she said. A thin smile crossed her narrow lips. It was such a weak attempt, she had such difficulty sustaining an expression of joy, I wondered when she'd last smiled even before Iskra's murder. She gazed past me toward a random place in space. "There was a time when he thought I was quite special. To think, I could have been Mrs. Simeon Simeonovich."

I seized the opportunity for conversation. "Where did the two of you meet?"

"At university. I was getting my master's degree in physics. Simmy was a doctoral candidate which basically made him an assistant professor. None of the tenured professors wanted to deal with graduate students after class. They delegated it to their favorite doctoral students. We hit it off right away."

I couldn't help but think of my deceased husband. He'd delegated all his grunt work to his favorite doctoral students, too. A
grungy-looking boy and the stunning female protégé with the
auburn hair. My sole encounter with her would persecute me until
the day I died.

"Why do you think you hit it off?" I said, my curiosity getting
the better of me. Maria frowned, and I immediately hit an apologetic note. "If you don't mind my asking. He's so mysterious, you
know?"

"Really?" Maria looked me over the way a woman did when
she imagined her former lover with another now. "How interesting, because I didn't think he was much of a mystery when I knew
him. He was ambitious and he was capable of being ruthless, but
he was a little boy at heart."

"How so?"

"His mother died when he was young. He was the kind of
man who needed a strong woman in his life. The kind of man who
was always looking for the approval of a strong woman. Has he
changed much, or is he still the way I describe?"

"I'm not sure I'm qualified to answer that."

"But you would like to become qualified, wouldn't you,
Nadia?"

I felt myself blushing and came within a split second of blurt-
ing out that what I really wanted to do was solve her daughter's
murder.

"I understand you work with the Salvation Army?" I said.

"Since back in Russia. We were the primary care system for
the homeless and the people infected with HIV. They're treated
like a leper class in Russia."

"Do you miss it?"

"Working with the homeless and the HIV-infected?"

"No. Russia."

Maria considered the question for a moment, looking every bit lucid and present. "Do I miss the Russian people? Absolutely. They are no different than the Dutch or the Americans, or anyone else. People are people. They want love, security and freedom. Their government lies to them – Putler took control of all three federal televisions stations less than a year after he took power – so they don't understand the world they live in. The Chekhists – the men and women who believe a secret police force should have unlimited powers – they control the entire country. And the people yield to them, out of loyalty and fear. It's a vicious cycle and they cannot break it, but the average Russian person is passionate, loyal and good."

"I believe that," I said, sincerely. "Speaking of Russian people … what can you tell me about *Nashi*?"

"Thugs," Maria said, with extreme prejudice.

"Why do you say that? I thought they were like a youth group with patriotic overtones."

"Who told you this nonsense? Is that what American believe?"

"Americans have never heard of *Nashi*. George told me Iskra had been a member. He made it sound like a normal extracurricular school activity."

"Sure, if you consider hooliganism a normal extracurricular school activity."

"Really?"

"Don't listen to anything my husband tells you. He's a Chekhist, too. How do you think we ended up with a home like this? He thinks Putler walks on water. He's such a fool. And the funniest thing of all is that he's not even a full-blooded Russian."

"You're kidding me."

Maria laughed. "He's a mutt. Part Russian, Moldovan, Belarusian, and Ukrainian. There's even a touch of Azeri in his past, but don't tell him that."

I couldn't help but smile before getting back on track. "But hooliganism? That doesn't sound like Iskra, based on what I've been able to learn about her."

"It wasn't. *Nashi* was created by the Kremlin to be the opposite of a freedom fighting organization with grass roots. Any politician dares to question the party line, *Nashi* follows him. Harasses him. Makes him look like a villain in public, on the internet. And if any community or university dares to organize a rally for democracy or any other worthy cause the State doesn't like . . ."

I raised my eyebrows.

"Nashi has an elite street fighting unit."

"Sanctioned by the Kremlin?" I said.

"They smash heads, especially talking heads." Maria frowned at me. "As though there's something going on in Russia that isn't sanctioned by the Kremlin?"

I shrugged.

"No, *Nashi* was not good for my daughter. She did not fit in with them. She was an artistic girl. She wanted to be free to express herself, and all that experience did was alienate her from her father, from me, and from Russia."

"I assume it was her father who made her join in the first place?"

"Of course. Like I said, he's a fool. He never understood our daughter. He only understood what kind of daughter he wanted to have, what kind of girl he thought she should be."

"And who was that?"

"The Chekhist's dream girl. An Olympic hero with uncommon beauty who marries a younger version of himself."

The notion of Iskra marrying created an opening for me. "Did Iskra have many boyfriends?"

"Too many, don't you think?"

"I wouldn't know."

"Of course you know. You've been working on this case long enough, and you're obviously an intelligent woman. George said you're smart. He said you were smart and that I would like you."

I wanted to make fun of her husband's compliment by reminding Maria she'd called him a fool twice, but I didn't dare.

"I'm trying to understand if there were any special men in her life that I don't know about," I said.

"She had many clients but no real lovers. Do you understand that?"

I lowered my head. "I'm so sorry …" I considered the question I was about to ask and made sure I needed to ask it. "What about women?"

Maria's face went blank. I feared she'd fallen into her personal abyss but then she frowned. "Excuse me?"

"If there were no special men in her life, is it possible there was a special woman in her life?"

Her lips quivered for a few seconds, and then tightened. "Are you suggesting my daughter – my Iskra – was a *lesbyanka*?"

I shook my head. "Not at all. Please don't be offended. I'm just being a professional, asking every possible question to consider every possible angle. You're a professional. Surely you understand."

She sipped her tea and collected herself. "Yes, you're quite right. Good for you. Not ruling out the ridiculous shows how diligent you are. George was right. You are very smart. Iskra a *lesbyanka*." She followed up with some laughter but it sounded forced, the creation of a mother who was in denial.

"How long did you know Iskra was moonlighting in *De Wallen*?" I said.

Maria didn't acknowledge me. Instead, she kept staring into space as though she'd withdrawn from our conversation again.

"George told me he only learned of what she was doing a couple of weeks before her death," I said.

"A few weeks ago, yes," she said, like a robot.

"I'm sorry to ask but this may be important. Did you confront Iskra about her night job? Did you try to talk her out of it?"

"You know, this tea needs a bit of sweetening."

"The reason I ask is if you had a mother-daughter conversation recently, you might have spoken about her life in general. She might have told you what was on her mind. She might have told you she was scared of someone. No, not scared, terrified. Did Iskra tell you that she was terrified of someone during her last few weeks? Or ever, for that matter?"

I was so focused on presenting my question in the most respectful way possible that I didn't see what was happening right before my eyes. Maria Romanova was spooning raspberry jam into her tea. She dragged her teaspoon around in circles, licked it, and batted her eyes twice in satisfaction. Then she sipped her tea.

"Ah," she said, "that's much better." Her eyes settled on me and she frowned. "Oh, hello. Remind me, dear. Who are you again?"

I didn't know what to say. I smiled, waited three beats, and introduced myself all over again. When I finished, she didn't respond with any sort of recognition.

"What was it you wanted to talk about this morning?" she said.

"Fear," I said. *When finesse fails, reach for the velvet hammer.* "We were talking about Iskra and the person she was mortally afraid of. You were about to tell me that person's name."

Maria Romanova almost smiled. "Iskra," she said, as slowly as one could utter two syllables. Then she came alive like an old engine that had finally turned over a sufficient number of times. "Fear, you say? My Iskra had no fear. None whatsoever. That was her gift. That was her tragedy. You understand, yes? Come. Let me show you some pictures."

I wasn't sure if she was entirely present again or not. Nevertheless, I followed her to a table by the window that contained a collection of framed photographs. The frames matched the pistachio color of the walls. Maria showed me a series of pictures of Iskra in chronological order. She supplemented each viewing with a commentary about her daughter at the given age.

I listened closely enough to comprehend the gist of Maria's remarks but tried hard to focus primarily on the images. The circumstances at the time a picture is snapped often dictate a subject's emotions. A joyous occasion might stimulate a smile from the most somber of people, while a comedic moment could jolt a manic depressant into smiling for a brief moment. Some people were born posers and didn't need any help. They could primp and preen their way to hide their true state of mind regardless of the adversity they might be suffering. And others still were the exact opposite – they remained transparent and uninterested in masking their inner selves.

Iskra Romanova was clearly one of the latter and her proud mother was clearly delusional. As she framed each photo with a memory of the specific time and place, Maria seemed to be describing the sweet-looking girl that could be seen in pictures until she turned twelve. From that point on her daughter looked increasingly sullen as the years passed. I paid special attention to her eyes. Anger, resentment and ultimately, disinterest defined their expression, until I saw the most recent picture.

In that photo, Iskra stood posing with her parents and Sasha in front of the famous I Amsterdam sign near a museum. They were all smiling, even Iskra. In fact, she appeared downright joyous. I wondered if her blissful state was a function of the romantic delusion that gripped her before her death.

"Who took this photo?" I said, lifting it up for closer examination.

Maria peered over my shoulder. "A stranger. We went to the Rijksmuseum to see an exhibition of Rembrandt's Claudius Civilis. I forced my family to pose for a picture so I could remember the moment. You know what they say. If you keep staring at a photograph, eventually you'll see things you never saw before. I don't remember ever seeing Iskra as happy as she was then."

"And when was this taken?"

"I don't remember exactly. Two or three weeks ago? It's the most recent picture I have of my Iskra."

Maria's estimate suggested the picture had been taken shortly before Iskra's murder, at the precise time when she'd fallen in love with Sarah Dumont.

"Who's the boy?" I said, pretending I didn't know, to see where the question led.

Maria glanced at me sharply. "You know who he is."

My face started to burn. All of a sudden Maria sounded more than lucid – she seemed downright perceptive.

"I do?" I said, denying her assertion because I didn't know what else to do.

"Yes, you do," she said, narrowing her eyes as though studying me for the first time. "George told me he showed you his picture and that you asked about him …"

"Oh my God …" I said, with an expression of shock.

"And that he arranged for you to meet with——"

"Sasha," I said, beaming at her.

She pursed her lips as though I was a poor actress. I, of course, refused to yield. I was certain I was a damned good one, especially when dressed in a lime green bikini in red-light districts that featured poor lighting.

"I didn't recognize him without his red Rasta hat and dreadlocks," I said.

Maria frowned. "His what?"

I nodded at the picture where Sasha wore his hair at shoulder length in its naturally greasy state for all to see.

"When I met him, Sasha was not ... Sasha," I said. "In fact, he didn't look anything like this."

"Eh?"

Maria hadn't seen her surrogate son in quite some time, or she'd have understood what I was talking about. Neither had George, I inferred. Sasha's Rasta get-up was so eccentric that it would have stimulated instant gossip between husband and wife regardless of what else was going on in their lives. I was as certain of this as they both were that their surrogate son was innocent in any wrongdoing in their daughter's murder.

"George used that same phrase when he first told me Sasha's name. 'Sasha is ... Sasha,'" I said. "It's like a family mantra where he's concerned. What exactly do you mean by that?"

Maria shrugged. "He's a dreamer. Always was, always will be. Some boys want to be men but they never learn how. And that is why we say Sasha ... is Sasha."

"Why do you say he's a dreamer?"

"Just that. He's always hatching one scheme or another to try to make his fortune, as opposed to going to school, getting a job, and working for a living. Now it's these silly t-shirts that look like something a six year-old could design. Before that it was his reggae band, and before that it was the acting."

"Acting?"

"We paid for three years of lessons. He actually had talent. He got three roles in local plays, but he wanted to star in movies and when it didn't happen right away he quit. No patience. No vision. He even had an agent but he lost his temper with him and burned that bridge, too."

I was surprised to hear that Sasha had a temper. This revelation forced me to consider the possibility that Sasha had been acting when we'd met, that he wasn't as sweet and honest as he'd appeared to be.

I studied every square inch of the picture again, as though I were looking at it for the first time. Iskra looked so different, so damn happy. That made this the most important picture of all, I thought, and made me wonder if there was anything else noteworthy about it. I studied her parents, Sasha, the people on the foreground and background, and even the signs around the museum, but found nothing out of the ordinary. My refusal to give up surprised me. I wasn't sure if my instincts were telling me that I was missing a clue that was staring me in the face or I was becoming desperate and searching for something that wasn't there.

"You said you think Iskra was afraid of something," Maria said.

"Not something. Someone."

"Does she looked frightened in this picture?" Maria said.

I glanced at Iskra yet again. There was no doubt about it. I wasn't misinterpreting. She looked uncharacteristically radiant and stress-free.

"I'd say she looks anything but frightened," I said.

"That's my girl," Maria said, smiling wistfully at the photo.

"But you must admit that she looks troubled in these other pictures." I pointed to the series of photos that captured the time period from earliest childhood to the final shot of her. "Is it possible that someone did something to allay her fears right before she was killed?"

A flicker of consternation crossed Maria's face, as though she knew that Iskra had been terrified of someone. But it vanished just as quickly, no doubt an unbearable reminder of her daughter's true disenchantment.

"George said you'd be persistent, that you would ask difficult questions, and that I should be happy about it. He said you're our best chance of finding Iskra's killer. He said the Dutch police –

they don't give a damn about a dead Russian girl. But I've just about had it with your rudeness. You tell me she was scared, I tell you she wasn't. But you just won't listen to me——."

"I'm so sorry," I said. "I don't mean to appear disrespectful. I'm just trying to reconcile what you're telling me with what other people told me."

"What other people?"

"And those people – at least one of them – saw her on a regular basis. One of them worked with her and insisted that she was terrified of someone——"

"Who said that? That disgusting brute? The one that was supposed to guard her and used her body instead? What does he call himself, the Greek?"

"The Turk?"

"Yes, that's the one. He gives all Greeks and Turks a bad name."

"How do you know him?" I said. "Have you met him? Personally?"

"Of course I know him. I knew all the people in my daughter's life."

"When and where did you meet him?"

Maria Romanova frowned as though she had no idea, or more likely, was falling into one of her trances and losing the gist of our conversation. I quickly spoke up to keep her on point, desperate for her to stay in the moment until she helped me flesh out this unexpected revelation.

"The Greek," I said, "as you called him ...

She continued staring into space. I cursed under my breath and tried to will her to focus on me.

"Did you meet him in *De Wallen*?" I said.

I emphasized the last two words thinking the name of the red-light district where her deceased daughter had been employed might resemble the sound of fingernails scraping a blackboard to her mother's ears.

But it had no such effect. Instead, my reference to Iskra's choice of vocations served only to immerse Maria into a deeper fog.

"Or did you run into him at Iskra's apartment, when he was walking her home one evening?" I said.

Maria's eyes regained perspective and focused in on me. "How did you know that?"

"What happened?"

"Nothing happened. We're not savages. Iskra introduced him as her bodyguard at work and the man was actually polite. He waited for George to offer his hand and then shook it – he even called me Mrs. Romanov."

"He was polite? Then I don't understand—"

"He wasn't so polite when George paid him a visit the next day," Maria said.

I took a half step back. "George met with the Turk?"

Maria nodded.

"Alone?" I said.

She nodded again.

That was interesting, I thought, because Maria's expression suggested she was recalling a bad memory.

"Where? In *De Wallen*?" I said.

"I think so."

"How did George find him?"

"I don't know. You'd have to ask George that. All I know is that George found out he was taking advantage of Iskra – using her for his own pleasure – and put an end to that. The thought of that disgusting man with our daughter …"

The Turk had been honest about receiving payment-in-kind instead of money from Iskra in exchange for acting as her occasional bodyguard. I suspected Maria knew this and had altered her interpretation of history to suit her needs and create a hero – the carefree and joyful daughter of her imagination – and a villain – the thug who'd used her body for pleasure.

"If we were still in Russia, I don't know what George would have done to that man."

The irony was that if the Romanovs hadn't left Russia, I thought, their daughter would still be alive. In Iskra's case, the great personal freedom and liberal social norms Amsterdam bestowed on its citizens had facilitated a lifestyle that had helped shorten her life.

"What did George do with him?" I said.

"Eh?"

"Obviously he was angry. And we're in the Netherlands, not Russia. So what did George do with the Turk?"

Maria Romanova shrugged. "He did the only thing he could do."

"Which was?"

"He paid him."

"To do what?"

"In cash," Maria said.

"He paid him in cash to do what?"

"Stay away from her."

I shook my head. "I'm so sorry he did that."

Maria looked surprised. "Why are you sorry?"

"Because as hard as it is to believe, the Turk really takes his job seriously. And he took his job protecting Iskra seriously."

Moisture appeared in the corner of Maria's eyes. It was the first time I'd seen the formation of tears since I'd arrived. Then the vacuous look returned to her face. After a moment of silence, she smiled demurely and asked me to remind her of my name.

I told her who I was, thanked her for her hospitality, and left.

When I'd first arrived I'd noted her palpable melancholy and her undernourished state, and thought that she looked as though she'd been unhappy for a long time. My visit hadn't shed any light on the source of her sadness, beyond her daughter's murder, but I had a strong gut feel based on my personal experiences with him and my own deceased husband.

When a married woman is suffering from depression, the husband is always a man of interest.

CHAPTER 16

The sauna occupied a nook in the middle of a commercial street no more than ten blocks from *De Wallen*. The proprietor obviously suffered from severe homesickness and a lack of originality because he'd named it Red Square. The entrance was sandwiched between a juice place and a travel agency, which suggested the establishment could appeal to a criminal on the lam – he could relax in the sauna, rehydrate with a smoothie, and then make arrangements to get the hell out of town.

A dilapidated sign hung over a door with peeling red paint. A doorbell no larger than a thimble protruded from the wall to the right – the bulb that was supposed to illuminate the button had either died or had been detached. The frontage was so narrow and unremarkable that one would never notice it unless she was absolutely looking for it. Given the sauna was frequented by a Russian minority that was less than cherished by the indigenous folk, I doubted its lack of visibility was accidental.

I'd called George Romanov as soon as I'd left his wife's house and told him I needed to speak with him. I wanted to debrief him about his visit with the Turk, and ask him why he hadn't told me about his meeting with him in the first place. I didn't mention my motives when I called, however, so that I could study his face later when I confronted him with what I knew. Instead I told him that I'd visited with Maria, which he knew to be the truth because he'd set up the meeting, and that I wanted to confirm some facts with him. He, in turn, acted as though he really were my best friend and made himself immediately available to me. I told him I had no interest in a sauna, but he informed me that I had no choice. He was leaving Amsterdam on business, he said, and this would be my last chance to see him for several days.

You will love it. If Americans frequented the banya, he said, they would shed their aggressions more readily and there would be less war in the world. I countered by telling him that I doubted his thesis was confined to my nation. He seemed to like that, because he chuckled and told me he'd be waiting for me in the lounge in his robe. That did not make me happy, because the thought of being near George Romanov with only one article of clothing on his body made my stomach turn. I could so easily picture him finding a reason to take it off in my presence.

But I had a job to do so what choice did I have? Besides, I was the rich man's friend and employee and Romanov knew that, right?

That's what I told myself as I marched along a dark and narrow corridor to the barebones front desk. A simultaneously fat and skinny attendant grabbed a white terry robe and an equally worn towel from a shelf behind him.

"The woman's dressing room is to the left," he said in Russian, and thrust the goodies in my direction.

I snorted a laugh before I could stop myself, so humorous did I find his assumption that I was going to remove one article of clothing from my body.

He was speaking Russian even though we were in Amsterdam and I hadn't spoken a word to him. This told me something.

"You know who I am," I said.

He grinned as though this confirmed his membership in Mensa, continuing to offer me the robe and towel as though he knew that it was just a matter of time before I accepted them. The arrogance of these Russians in Amsterdam, I thought. And the self-delusion, too.

"Mr. Romanov described you to me," he said.

"Oh, really? What did he say about me?"

"He said that I'd know who you were within a minute."

"How so?" I said.

"Two reasons. When we get new guests, they're mostly men visiting from Russia. Not too many women besides the locals."

I knew Romanov had to have given him a more personal description of me, most likely something I'd find brutally offensive. This in, in turn, would make me loathe him even more, a prospect which brought me a certain measure of glee.

"And what was the second reason?" I said.

"He said you would ask me how I knew who you were right away."

The attendant broadened his grin.

Son-of-a-bitch, I thought. That was a pretty good line by Romanov, which I didn't appreciate. The last thing I wanted was to start liking him for any reason whatsoever.

I glanced at the robe and towel in the attendant's hands and shook my head.

"No sauna for me," I said. "George said he'd meet me in the lounge."

"No one's allowed in the lounge in street clothes."

"Really?" I said. "What are you going to do, call the police to have me arrested for wearing street clothes?"

The attendant shook his head, looking completely serious. "You and I," he said. We're Russian. The police won't help us so there's no sense in calling them. Mr. Romanov said that if he sees you in street clothes, he's going to walk out. Said he won't talk to you at all."

"Why?"

"Because no one is allowed in street clothes in the lounge. Club policy. You can see why, can't you? Street clothes ... it looks like business. People come in here, they want to leave business behind. They only want to be with other people who are leaving business behind."

I rolled my eyes.

The attendant extended his arms fully, practically placing the robe and towel in my arms. His grin broadened into a full fledged smile.

I took the robe and towel and headed into to the women's dressing room. Score one for the arrogant and self-deluded, I thought, before deciding that such a description was equally applicable to me, at least in this case.

The dressing room needed minor renovations, the way a salvage yards needs a facelift. Old carpet smell was winning the war against the room deodorizer and winning ugly. The vanity and toilets were technically clean but the fixtures were so old and rusty that the areas looked dirty anyways. A poorly aging matron gave me a disproving onceover as she gathered wet towels from a basket and stuffed them into her bin for washing. After her eyes met mine she glanced at the tip jar beside the hair drier. I ignored her and the tip jar without suffering any guilt because she hadn't done anything special for me, and because I was from New York. The minute you crossed into one of the City's five boroughs, someone had his hand in your pocket – picking one's spots to express gratitude was a constant exercise in financial self-preservation.

I changed into the robe, whose threads had seen their better days. There was just enough terry cloth to cover my ass when I sat down on the bench in the dressing room. After a brief moment of fury, I marched back into the lobby and asked the attendant for a longer robe. He chuckled, obliged and my spirits brightened a bit.

I walked out to the lounge with a towel slung over my shoulders just in case I needed to cover a seat. I expected to see a bunch of rich old Russian men and the prototypical collection of shapely swizzle sticks that stirred their drinks when they were apart from their wives. Instead I found Romanov sitting alone in a recliner beside a huge Jacuzzi, three retirees reading papers in a seating area against a wall, and two handsome young men playing cards at a bar. The latter were dressed head to toe in white, like male nurses.

Romanov stood up to greet me. He looked affable, not angry and not trying too hard to be polite, either. In fact, he looked genuinely pleased to see me.

"Do you want a massage?" he said.

I hesitated because I feared he might be making a pass at me. But I was wrong. Romanov maintained an earnest if not genuinely gracious expression as he pointed with open palm toward the two studs in white uniform.

"If you're suffering from stress," Romanov said, "the boys will work wonders on you. They are licensed and serious. This is no cheap provocation, I can assure you."

"I didn't think it was," I said, which of course, was untrue. I had no idea what to think. "I'm good, thank you."

I covered the bottom of a rattan chair with my towel. The chair shared a side table with Romanov's recliner. We took our seats, facing each other at an angle, not entirely head-on, which presented a problem. I wouldn't be able to see his entire facial expression as I questioned him. So I quickly shifted my chair so that I could see him better.

"What are you doing?" he said, rushing over to help me.

"Just rearranging our seats a bit so we can see each other better," I said. "Unless, of course, the sight of my American legs offends you."

He stole an approving glance at my calves, still tanned from my undercover exploits in *De Wallen*. "Well, now that you put it that way ... Let me get you a glass of lemon water. Very good for the immune system."

The intensity of his reaction to the simple act of moving a chair suggested that he wasn't merely concerned that I was a performing a task that a gentleman should perform for a lady, but that I'd upset the lounge's feng shui. But the lounge was unlikely to be featured in Architectural Digest, with its cracked tile floor and used beach furniture. I recalled Romanov's fastidious appearance at Stout! and how properly his clothes fit his remarkably well-toned physique. There was no doubt that he had a strong sense of the proper order of things and he liked them arranged accordingly.

"Was my wife helpful?" he said, after he returned.

"She was," I said. "Thank you so much for setting that up."

"Don't mention it. Emotions run high but all three of us want the same thing here, don't we?"

"To be honest with you, I don't want to appear rude of indelicate but she seemed ..."

"Disoriented?" Romanov said.

"Forgive me. I know this is a very difficult time. I mention it only because it would have been inconsiderate of me not to mention it."

"Say no more. I know you mean well. Maria has had a trying life. Her sister and her husband were found guilty of embezzlement at a Russian bank last year and have been sentenced to jail for six years. She thinks they're being held accountable for our move to Holland by Russian authorities who wish we'd kept all our assets in Russia as opposed to London, and were paying taxes there as opposed to avoiding them here. But that is a figment of her imagination. Those same authorities are the ones who've siphoned the most capital out of Russia and into places like London. And besides, President Putler and I are good friends."

"That's interesting," I said.

"Why is that interesting?"

"Because Simmy's a good friend of President Putler's, too."

"Of course he is. The President made him, gave him his start."

"That's not what I heard," I said, telegraphing the disappointment in my voice. It was one thing to offend me, but an entirely different one when you offended my friend. "I was told he bought his first plant fare and square."

"Yes," Romanov said. "At auction."

"Exactly."

"At an auction of one."

"Oh, come now," I said. "That can't possibly be, even in Russia."

"Fine. I'm sure there was more than one bidder. And I'm sure none of them were deemed to have the necessary financial resources to help the asset grow the Russian economy. Only the PhD student without a ruble to his name could do that."

I took of sip of lemon water to boost my immune system and divert my mind from the nonsense spewing from Romanov's mouth.

"I'll have to ask him about this some day," I said. "Don't worry, I won't quote you."

Romanov shrugged. "Feel free to tell him I told you this. It will be the equivalent of telling him that I told you that the lemon water is good for your constitution. It's not an original thought. It's common knowledge."

Romanov spoke so calmly and with such conviction that I found myself hoping lemon was detrimental to my constitution.

"You're upset," he said.

"Of course I am."

"Because Simeonovich is your client and your friend."

"No. I have no friends. I'm upset because I revealed my emotions to you. And as an investigator and a woman who prides herself on being inscrutable, that's unacceptable. You see?"

Romanov burst out laughing and slapped his knee. "That's fantastic. The second you said you were Ukrainian, I knew we'd be friends for life. I knew it."

I grinned and nodded in agreement, visions of Ukrainian troops absorbing mortar shells from Russian soldiers posing as some sort of bullshit separatists dancing in my imagination. *Oh, yes. We were friends for life.*

And now it was time for my best friend to tell me exactly what I wanted to know, so I turned solemn as a prelude to my segue. It took no effort because I had nothing against his wife.

"I'm just relieved to hear you know about Maria and it wasn't something that I did."

"No, no," he said. "Don't you dare blame yourself, not for a moment. I'm her husband, how could I not know? And don't worry. It's not the onset of any form of dementia, even though it may seem that way. She's under a doctor's care. A Dutchman. Tops in his field. Transient global amnesia, he says, brought on by stress, anxiety and confusion."

The last word surprised me because I expected to hear "depression" instead. But then, it made sense that Maria Romanova might be confused. After all, she was the mother of a college girl turned sex worker suddenly involved in a same-sex romance with no previous signs of such inclinations. All of that was accurate except the tense of the verb, I thought. Her daughter had been all those things before she'd been butchered to death.

Those images inspired by the crime scene – they never strayed far from consciousness.

"Maria told me you met Iskra's bodyguard," I said. "The Greek fellow."

Romanov appeared confused.

"The one that calls himself the Turk."

Confused turned to surprise. "Is he really Greek?"

I shrugged. "So he told me."

Romanov mused out loud. "You wonder why a man would do that to himself."

"Do what?"

"Put himself in a position where he's his own mortal enemy. How can a Greek who calls himself the Turk ever be happy?"

"But he was happy," I said. "At least for a while, wasn't he?"

Romanov didn't blink or blanch. "If you mean while he was working for Iskra and getting paid in a manner that would shame any father, I'm sure he was."

"Why didn't you tell me about him when we had lunch?"

Romanov seemed genuinely perplexed. "For what reason? He liked my daughter. I met the man. I spoke with him. He was employed by the people who run the room she rented. As disgusting as it all was, he was a professional."

"That you went back to see privately and had words with——"

"You can't possibly be thinking he's a suspect."

"Why not?"

"Because he's a good man."

Romanov's words caught me by surprise.

"The Turk is a good man?" I said.

"Absolutely. I went to his work place, which is to say I went to Iskra's old office and had a discussion with him."

"A discussion?"

Romanov nodded. "A father to friend-of-his-daughter type of discussion."

"After which you paid him to go away."

Romanov shook his head. "On the contrary. That's what I told Maria to simplify matters for her and to get her to stop worrying about him."

"You mean you didn't have a confrontation? You didn't pay him to go away?"

"Why would I pay him to go away when he was protecting her? My impression is, he takes his job seriously. You've met him. What do you think?"

"That it's a shame he wasn't with her twenty-four seven or she might still be alive."

"Then we're agreed on that."

"You did a great job. Maria was so convinced you paid someone off to stay away."

"I didn't pay anyone, but I had a discussion with someone. It just wasn't the Turk."

I leaned forward. "Who was it then?"

"The cop that was totally obsessed with her."

"A cop?"

"The one that was paying for her services and stalking her at all hours."

"A cop was doing that?" I said. "That's incredible. What's his name?"

"He's the detective. The one investigating the case." Romanov's face contorted into a mask of pure hate. "You met him at Iskra's apartment. Goes by the name of De Vroom."

CHAPTER 17

I called De Vroom and told him I had valuable information pertinent to his investigation of Iskra's murder. That was not a lie. That my discoveries concerned him and his alleged relationship with Iskra didn't render them any less relevant. De Vroom insisted I meet with him right away even though it was his day off.

As I headed for our rendezvous, I experienced doubts about my personal safety for the first time. I'd been nervous when the police had slapped the cuffs on me and locked me in a cell, but I'd never feared my life was at risk. The prospect of dealing with a cop that was anything less than one hundred percent scrupulous, however, left me believing that I should be legitimately shaken up. But I wasn't, and that in turn, is what really shook me up. Deep down, I knew I should have been more reluctant to pursue my investigation but I couldn't seem to stop myself.

The mitigating factor to my concern was De Vroom's choice of venues. He couldn't have proposed a safer place to meet excluding the United States Embassy and Simmy's armored yacht. That included the police station, since I was no longer entirely certain I could trust the Dutch cops.

The Cupcake Whisperer doubled as a cake store that also offered lessons in baking. Among their curricula were family-oriented sessions including one for cupcake decoration. I waited for De Vroom outside the gingerbread-like building, studying the scene through the front window. A swarm of mothers surrounded a room full of enchanted children, frosting and candies all over the place. Among the mothers sat one solitary and disturbingly handsome police detective, flanked by identical twin daughters in pink dresses.

I wasn't any good at guessing little kids' ages. All I knew for certain was that they were young enough to be totally adorable and not nearly old enough to fathom what one human being was capable of doing to another.

I texted De Vroom to glance out the window, and enjoyed watching him read my message, knowing that he was about to glance my way any second. But he didn't, cool and handsome bastard that he was. Instead, he read the note and strolled over to a sweet-looking mother and exchanged a few words with her. The mother glanced at De Vroom's girls as though he'd asked her to watch over them and nodded with a dazzling smile thrown in to-boot. As he headed toward the door, the woman sauntered over to the girls and chatted with them about their cupcakes. The woman and De Vroom's children's warm facial expressions and relaxed mannerisms suggested they knew each other. Given the woman's classic beauty, I wasn't surprised De Vroom was acquainted with her.

He arrived looking formidable and alluring at the same time.

"I thought I told you to leave Amsterdam," he said.

"For my own safety," I said. "And you were very thoughtful when you said it, as though you cared about me."

"I do care about you. It's my job to care about all people in Amsterdam, including the tourists. But you're still here, which makes me wonder if you care about yourself."

"I care about my job more than I care about myself. That's what's known as being a professional."

"No," De Vroom said. "That's what's known as being an American. Can we go for a walk? Before my girls start wondering if I'm interviewing new mommies for them. And for the record, that's their choice of language."

We strolled along the sidewalk on the shady side of the road. Cars passed us at a brisk pace. There was no one walking within earshot but a few pedestrians could be seen on both sides of the street. I took comfort from my observation that we weren't alone.

"Where's their real mommy?" I said.

"She's dead," De Vroom said, matter-of-factly.

"Oh my God," I said under my breath, without even thinking, horrified by my presumptuousness and stupidity. "I'm so sorry, Detective."

"The name is Erik."

I'd just assumed he was divorced. He was an attractive man with an incredibly stressful job. He and his twin girls were a magnet for the bevy of Dutch beauties at the cupcake place. If he'd been married before but wasn't married anymore, he had to be divorced. He was too young to be a widower.

Except he wasn't. Anyone old enough to be married was old enough to have buried a spouse. No one knew than better than I did.

"I'm sorry for your loss, Eric."

I wondered if she'd died from an illness, or an unfortunate accident of some kind.

De Vroom was a detective. He didn't need me to ask the question to know what I was thinking.

"Malaysia Airlines flight seventeen," he said.

I was even more stunned than when he'd told me his wife was dead. I'd mentioned the airplane tragedy at the police station to convince him I could help him gather intelligence about Iskra's murder from Amsterdam's Russian community. During our conversation, De Vroom had remained mute. I thought he'd stayed mum in the spirit of the negotiation we were conducting about the terms of my release from custody. It had never occurred to me that he'd suffered a personal loss in the tragedy.

"Amsterdam to Kuala Lumpur," he said, repeating the words I'd spoken to him. "One of those two-hundred and eighty-three passengers that the Russians killed was my wife. She was a vice president for an agricultural technology company on a business trip to Malaysia. She'd struck a deal with the country to advise them on stepping up their agricultural production. Vegetable seedlings – that was her specialty."

"Now I feel terrible that I ever brought it up ... that flight ... when we first met ..."

"You mean when you were in jail?"

I spied a grin on his face and smiled to be agreeable and out of sheer relief that we were laughing about something.

"Right," I said.

"How could you have known? Don't worry about it. You said you have some new information. Let's have it."

"I met with George Romanov——"

"So you are working for the family."

"I can neither confirm nor deny that assertion."

"If you want to learn to deny, no better teacher than a Russian——"

"And he told me that he was certain – that he had irrefutable evidence that Iskra had a client who took a particular interest in her."

"I know all about that client," De Vroom said. "And so do you. She drives a Porsche Macan and lives in Bruges. I've met with Sarah Dumont and spoken with her. She cooperated fully and she's not a suspect. Have you met her?"

"I have."

"And?"

"She's innocent where the murder is concerned, though in all other matters I doubt that description applies."

"We obviously met the same woman. So if you agree she's innocent in Iskra's murder, how could Romanov have told you something about her that you think is so important?"

"He didn't."

"I don't understand."

"He told me about another one of her clients that was even more infatuated with her."

"Another woman?"

"I suspect there were other women," I said.

"Well, that was her business, right? So which one was it that Romanov said was obsessed with her? Who was she? What was her name?"

"She is a he. And his name is Eric De Vroom."

De Vroom had steered me toward the building-side of the sidewalk after we started walking, choosing to walk along the street himself. This was standard operating procedure for a European gentleman, protecting the lady from the splash of a tire powering through a puddle or a stray elbow from a bicyclist. At least that's what my father had taught me. But his position also gave him leverage in case he wanted to permanently shut my mouth by shoving me sideways into an alley, such as the one that was opening up right before me—

We passed the entrance to the alley without incident.

"Romanov misinformed you," De Vroom said.

"So you deny having a relationship with Iskra?"

"Absolutely not."

"You don't deny it?" I said.

"Why would I deny the truth?"

"Now I'm the one who doesn't understand."

De Vroom shrugged, not a hint of discomfort, let alone guilt, in his voice or carriage. "I had a relationship with her the way you have one with any professional. But to say I was obsessed with her – that's ridiculous. It sounds like something an angry father made up. An angry Russian father who's got a vendetta against the Dutch, especially the detective who hasn't solved his daughter's murder."

I stopped walking because I wanted to make sure I was hearing him correctly. "But you admit you had a professional relationship with her?"

"Of course. Why not?"

"You had sex with her for money."

"I'm sure that hurts your American ears," De Vroom said.

"You have no idea."

"You're a repressed country with your Christian-Judeo values. Iskra Romanova and I made a series of transactions within the law as consenting adults."

"Romanov said that it was more than a series of transactions. He said he had it on good authority that you were hanging around her office on your off days." I glanced at him and thought of his two daughters. "Erik ... they said you were stalking her."

"Good authority? Romanov must have talked to the Turk. He's actually a good guy but he's not the smartest man in the city. I might trust him as a bouncer if I owned a bar, but I wouldn't trust him as my sister's bodyguard. He only sees what he wants to see."

"Are you saying you were a mirage and you weren't really showing up at Iskra's office at all hours of the day, every day of the week?"

De Vroom appeared more amused than concerned about anything I had just told him.

"Did I show up at random hours? Sure. My schedule, with the job and the kids ... it fluctuates. But every day of the week ... come on, now. I'm not twenty years old anymore."

He laughed at himself, without pride, ego or concern that he could be proven to have been involved in Iskra's murder, or any wrongdoing whatsoever.

"It was a tough time for me," he said. "We all cope in different ways. For me, she turned out to be a tremendous outlet. She helped me find joy at a time when I was really struggling."

"You make her sound like a therapist, and based on everything we know, she's probably the one who needed therapy——"

"There's this spot at the base of the head of a man's penis. If you apply a certain amount of continuous pressure there, it results in the most excruciating and joyous tension a man can ever experience——"

"Okay, that's enough," I said. "I get the picture."

"If I'd told you I'd taken up handball or military-style morning boot camp, you would have thought that made perfect sense. Am I right?"

"Well ..."

"But using sex as a form of therapy – you probably have a moral issue with it."

"Does the police department not have a moral issue with you being the lead detective on the case given you——"

"Given I what?"

My voice rose. "Given you had a relationship with the victim."

"A professional relationship. There was nothing personal about it at all. So not only is there no conflict, I have an edge. I knew the victim, a bit about her habits and work place. I am the perfect lead for the case."

I stood dumbfounded for a moment, and then we resumed walking.

After a few steps, De Vroom appeared thoughtful as he mused out loud. "Iskra Romanova was an artist with a God-given talent."

"Sure," I said. "Like Van Gogh."

"Make fun of it all you like. You and I, we are both on this Earth for a very short time. I'm getting all the pleasure and joy that I can within the confines of what is moral and just. Are you?"

"I'm practicing delayed gratification."

"Maybe your pleasure is psychological while mine was physical," De Vroom said.

"What are you talking about?"

"Maybe having Mr. Simeon Simeonovich as your client provides you with the same kind of thrill that I experienced with Iskra."

My face flushed.

"A limousine picked you up when I released you from jail," he said. "Our camera caught the reflection of the man in the back seat in the side window when the driver opened the door for you to get inside. I traced the license plate. It belongs to a Danish subsidiary that's part of the Orel Group, a conglomerate owned by a Russian billionaire. When I found this man's photo on the internet, it matched the picture of the man in the back seat of the limo."

"I can neither confirm nor deny my client's identity."

"You're working for a Russian," he said. "And to the average cop, that would be reason enough not to trust you. But you and I, I think we're different. I think we've developed a certain relationship."

"Now you're scaring me, given the nature of some of your relationships ... "

"You and I know we shouldn't trust each other because it's our job to question everything and everyone and prepare for the unexpected. But deep down, I think we know we really can trust each other because we share a profound respect for one thing above all else."

"A properly decorated cupcake?"

"The truth," De Vroom said.

I had to agree with him. Perhaps I was a fool. Maybe he'd asked me to leave the country when he'd released me from jail so that I wouldn't investigate the murder. Not that he had any reason to fear me – I was nobody. But given I'd had the audacity to pose as a prostitute and he'd deduced that Simmy was my client, my stirring things up could only cause him problems if he were the murderer.

We took a right. His children appeared in front of the Cake Whisperer straight ahead, holding hands with the statuesque Dutch woman who had been taking care of them.

"So I'm going to tell you the truth," De Vroom said, "And when you walk away, you'll know that I'm as certain of it as I am that I love my children. If you ask me why I'm certain of it, I won't have an answer. I'll just tell you that's based on a feeling right here." He patted his gut with an open palm.

"Okay," I said. "You have my attention."

"A Russian committed the murder. The murder took place in their community and was committed by one of them."

I didn't pat my gut, nor could I explain why, but I had the exact same feeling.

CHAPTER 18

I watched De Vroom scoop up his girls, one in each arm, and extort a big kiss hello from them in front of the Cake Whisperer. He did not extort a similar kiss from the lovely woman who'd agreed to watch over his daughters, though she looked as though she wouldn't have minded if he had done so.

As the scene unfolded, I considered what I'd deduced from my interview with De Vroom. Iskra had lied and told Sasha that the Turk was obsessed with her to placate him when he pressed her to explain why she seemed so frightened. That was my previous conclusion and I still believed it. The person whom she feared was someone else.

And now I was confident that person wasn't De Vroom. He was a widower with two small children. And he was a cop, for God's sake. Unless he was a serial killer at large, which was basically a zero probability, why on Earth would he have committed such a gruesome murder, one that excised the same body parts that gave him so much pleasure?

No, I thought. Someone else had been even more obsessed with her, and that other person was the one that she'd feared, the one that had killed her. And she hadn't dared reveal that person's identity to Sasha, the Turk, Sarah Dumont, or anyone else.

After watching the family reunion, I bounded around the corner toward my hotel. A minute later, I received a text message from Simmy inquiring if I was available for dinner tonight. He wanted me to give him an update on the case. I responded in the affirmative, and after he told me when and where, I found myself comparing Simmy to De Vroom as eligible bachelors. There was no comparison whatsoever, of course, because one man was upset at the mere prospect of my impersonating a prostitute, while the other one frequented them with no remorse. There was the matter of money, too, and all the lifestyle and security that it afforded. Both of these matters were secondary to how a man made a woman feel about herself, because all the gold in the world couldn't compensate a woman for voluntarily entering or remaining in an abusive marriage. That I knew from personal experience.

A blur flashed on my left. Someone slammed into me.

I careened toward the right of the sidewalk, momentum taking me sideways, no idea what was happening.

A second blur appeared at my right.

I collided with a concrete statue. Except it wasn't a statue, it was a man, made of flesh, blood and bone, wearing a charcoal business suit. He grabbed me by the scruff of my collar as though I were his kitten, covered my mouth to muffle my screams with his other hand, and dragged me into an alley. The other blur caught up to us and grabbed my legs. Together they lifted me into the air and carried me deeper into the alley.

I thrashed with my arms and legs, tried to wriggle free and kick myself loose from my assailants but my efforts were to no avail.

Hadn't a pedestrian or a driver seen me?

The alley looked familiar, like the one I'd just passed with De Vroom.

De Vroom, I thought. He was less than a block away around the corner. If I could just break free ...

I kicked and thrashed again but accomplished nothing. I could see my assailants clearly now, both in nicely fitted suits and dark glasses, athletic men in the prime of their lives. They had square chins and blank stares.

A third man came out of nowhere and opened a door. This one had lines in his face and thinning hair. The other two brought me inside and third one closed the door behind us.

The room contained a collection of garbage barrels and bins, and maintenance tools such as brooms, blowers and snow shovels, and buckets of dirt and salt. It was the perfect place to deposit a corpse, I thought, and that was as much thinking as I was capable of mustering under the circumstances.

And the circumstances quickly unfolded to be among the most horrific I'd ever experienced.

The three men removed all my clothes.

They didn't say a word and they didn't touch my body in a provocative fashion. In fact, they seemed completely detached as though they were performing a standard procedure according to some sort of guide book. I would have taken a measure of comfort in this observation if I wasn't scared shitless that I was about to be violated and killed.

And then when I was naked, they let me slip out of their grasp and released me onto the ice cold cement floor. The hand that had been covering my mouth slipped away. I worked my lips and teeth free from stiffness, but I knew better than to risk incurring their cumulative wrath by screaming.

I scurried back against one of the garbage cans like a cat looking for a wall for protection and folded my arms over my breasts. But two of the men hoisted me up to my feet by my arms, exposing them again. And then the third man – the leader – opened a switchblade and placed the blade just beneath my left nipple.

"Such tits," he said, in fluent Russian.

I wanted to spit in his face, bury my fingernails in his eyes, and kick him in the balls, all at the same time. But I also wanted to survive this ordeal so I opted to keep my mouth shut instead.

"You're not safe in Amsterdam," he said. "Not in the daylight, not in the night time. We'll leave you your mobile so you can call the airline and go back to New York right away. If you don't there will be a next time. And if there's a next time, we'll leave you the phone again. Problem is, you won't have a tongue to speak with or fingers to use it. You see, one way or another, you're going to leave this country and not come back."

They stuffed me into one of the garbage bins, threw my cell phone and handbag inside, and wheeled me out into the alley. The sound of a bolt slamming shut and a key turning in a lock followed, and then I heard several sets of footsteps grow increasingly faint until the alley turned quiet.

I sat curled in the garbage trying not to vomit from the rancid smell of decaying foodstuff. Once I couldn't hear footsteps I counted to ten for good measure – as slowly as I could but undoubtedly faster than I realized – and then pushed up with all my might.

The hard plastic cover swung up and over the side. I stood up straight but there was no way for me to extricate myself from the bin – it was too tall for me to climb out, too narrow for me to swing my legs up. The air felt frigid against my naked, sweaty body. I could see daylight down at the end of the alley where a strip of sidewalk was visible. The thought of someone walking by and catching a glimpse of me, a living monument to disposable refuse, induced new found levels of self-loathing.

I deflected a bolt of anxiety and realized what I needed to do.

I rocked sideways back and forth until the bin toppled to the ground. I kept my head up, sustained a blow to my side and ribs, and slithered out of the can still breathing and without harming myself. Then I quickly closed the bin, rolled it against the wall and took cover behind it. Yes, I was squatting so that nothing other than my feet touched the concrete. No, there were no cardboard boxes, plywood remnants, or swaths of stray cloth conveniently available so that I could kneel, let alone an empty garbage bag that I could use to cover my body. The Dutch kept their country clean, even the back alleys.

Tears spilled from my eyes. Some women might have been embarrassed about this, but I was used to it. My brain released the water behind my eyes at a rate commensurate with my flow of adrenaline under adverse emotional circumstances. It didn't make me any less capable of conquering them. And as for appearances, any woman with a fresh face suffering my current fate was either professionally trained to handle such a situation or deeply troubled.

My decision tree flashed before me. The imaginary branches sprouted with alternative courses of action.

The mere exercise calmed my nerves and helped steady my breathing. Analyzing problems and finding solutions was my joy. This was home.

I always started from scratch, always began by avoiding the simplest of assumptions. I ruled out nothing.

Q1: Run out into the street naked and hope a kind person helps me?

A: High probability police are called no matter what explanation I give. If the police get involved, my mental health could be questioned given I've already been arrested for prostitution. Deportation possible to probable, interruption of my investigation highly likely.

Negative.

Q2: Call Simmy for help?

A: He's my client and he's Simmy. I'd rather die.

Negative.

Q3: Call De Vroom for help?

A: He's a cop accountable to his hierarchy with two kids who depend on the income his career provides. This time he might really have me thrown out of the country.

Negative.

Q4: Call hotel for help?

A: Hotel would need to cover its ass in case I'm a risk to myself, their other guests, or Amsterdam. High probability cops get involved, which is unfortunate because this solution is the easiest on my pride and ego.

Negative.

Q5: Who the else can I call?

A: The contrarian's solution. So unimaginable it must be the right move. The only person I know in Amsterdam whose opinion of me is irrelevant to me, and also someone I can be certain will not go to the police.

Analysis complete.

Solution found.

The only remaining question was whether my potential savior was still in the city.

CHAPTER 19

My hands shook as I checked my recent calls so I could reach out to the only man I was willing to ask for help. The odds were against me not only because he was scheduled to leave town but because that's how life is. The minute you start to want something desperately, it immediately becomes commensurately more difficult to obtain.

But sometimes you can get lucky, too, especially if you're the owner of a wicked losing streak.

My best friend in Amsterdam picked up on the third ring. I gave him the abbreviated truth without edits. He swore in Russian and told me he was on his way.

Twenty minutes later he appeared in the alley, rich leather overnight bag slung over his shoulder, dressed in a gray turtleneck and black driver's jacket. When he spoke my name I raised my hand so that he could see it over the garbage bin. Then I closed my eyes and tried to suppress my ego so that I could endure the humiliation of him seeing me in my current state.

But Romanov surprised me. He cringed when he found me behind the bin, averted his eyes, and began to remove the contents from his bag, all the while making soothing noises as though I were his daughter and he were my guardian, here to comfort and protect me. His emergency clothing kit was my dream ensemble for my predicament – a navy warm-up suit made of Italian cashmere and matching blue socks to boot. The New Balance shoes were a size too big, but in the grand scheme of things, more than useable. After I finished tying the laces, I stood up and marveled at how well the clothes fit. Only when I glanced at Romanov did I realized why – the former Olympic caliber diver and I were of similar stature.

He tried to wrap a blanket around me for added warmth before we left.

"No," I said. "I'm fine."

"Your teeth say otherwise," Romanov said. "They haven't stopped chattering since I found you."

"My teeth lie. Soon as I get home I'm going to have them replaced."

"You're in shock. Your body has been focused on staying alive. That means your immune system is compromised. You're susceptible to catching a cold, or worse. Put on this blanket. I will not have you getting sick on top of all you've been through, which you're going to tell me about in my car."

"No blanket," I said, and started to walk away from him. "If there's a cop and he sees me walking out of the alley, I might look strange. It could attract the wrong kind of attention."

In fact, I had no such worries. My refusal to drape the blanket over my body was simply a matter of pride.

I hurried toward the light at the end of the alley, leaving Romanov behind me. He caught up to me in a flash, leather bag in hand, and guided me toward his Mercedes SUV. It looked like a military jeep custom-made for the general who'd absconded with the treasure. I recognized the driver as one of the masseurs from the spa. He opened the back door and we climbed inside. Even after we were comfortably ensconced, however, the driver didn't get back behind the wheel. Instead he lit a cigarette and found a comfortable spot near an empty storefront. He remained near enough to watch over us but not so close as to be able to eavesdrop.

Romanov gave me a bottle of water, and I promptly drank half of it. Then I thanked him for coming to my rescue.

He waved his hand. "No need to thank a friend, especially not one who shares your ancestral heritage. But I can't believe the men who did this to you were Russian."

"They were."

"Well they weren't from Amsterdam, or even Holland. That I can promise you."

"How can you be so sure?" I said.

"Because I would have known. Nothing happens in my community without my knowing about it."

"Then they weren't from your community."

Romanov nodded once with conviction, leaving no doubt that his local stature was very important to him. "I'm glad you agree with me, because my next conclusion ... you aren't going to like that one very much."

"Now you've really got my attention," I said. "Because I have no idea what you're talking about."

"I know. That's because you're a bit blinded."

"Excuse me?"

"Infatuation can do that."

"What?"

"When a woman is infatuated with a man, she loses proper perspective. Even a woman of discipline and intelligence like you—"

"Whom exactly am I supposedly infatuated with?"

Romanov pulled his head back and pinched his lips as though I'd insulted him by not being open and honest with him.

"I'm not kidding," I said.

That was a lie, of course. I knew who he was talking about. I was just mortified that a relative stranger had inferred I had feelings for my client, or anyone else, for that matter.

"Simeonovich," Romanov said.

I waited for him to say more but he didn't.

"What about him?" I said.

"It's rather obvious, isn't it?"

"Obviously not to me. According to you, I'm infatuated with him."

"You admit it."

"I said 'according to you.'"

"But you didn't fool either of us," Romanov said. "Has it occurred to you that Simeonovich could be responsible for the attack on you today?"

I stared at Romanov for a moment, then looked away. I didn't want to insult the man who'd saved me by informing him that was the dumbest suggestion I'd heard in a long time.

"No, no," Romanov said. "I'm not suggesting he had a hand in it. Good God, no. I'm sure he has all the respect in the world for you. No, I mean has it ever occurred to you that these men attacked you because of something Simeonovich wants?"

"That's ridiculous," I said, but my voice trailed off as I followed Romanov's logic.

Someone had sent Russian thugs to get me out of Amsterdam, I thought. If that person was actually trying to impede Simmy's agenda, that meant he would gain by my departure. The only agenda Simmy and I shared in Amsterdam was Iskra's murder. This suggested that the person behind the attack on me would benefit from Iskra's murder not being solved. That in turn implied that solving Iskra's murder would somehow help Simmy above and beyond doing a favor for an old friend.

"Maybe, "Romanov said, "for reasons beyond our comprehension, Simeonovich's future depends on the resolution of

Iskra's murder. He's under political pressure, yes? Maybe my daughter's death and his future are connected."

"That's crazy," I said.

Romanov shrugged. "You're probably right. Note that I said 'probably.'"

"So noted," I said.

Romanov motioned through the window for his driver to return.

"If anyone can find out the truth for certain," Romanov said, "I'm sure it's you."

CHAPTER 20

Simmy met me at the Art'otel's swanky contemporary bar. Plush velvet chairs and sofas were arranged in secluded areas for maximum privacy. Dim lighting and a haunting tune from a Scandinavian female duet added to the seductive setting.

We ordered our drinks. Simmy made a predictable choice, opting for a single malt scotch that reeked of exclusivity and masculinity. I ordered a beer, a Heineken, to be specific. I hadn't had one in ages due to my fear of carbohydrates and love of the taste.

Simmy cast an equally predictable look of disapproval at me after the waiter left with our orders.

"Don't tell me," I said. "A woman should never drink beer. It's not ladylike."

"It most certainly is not," Simmy said, "but that doesn't mean it's not provocative. When a woman participates in a masculine activity, it can be ... how shall I put it?"

"Sexy?" I said.

Simmy gave me the slightest shrug in agreement.

"And drinking beer is a masculine activity?" I said.

"The laborers who built the Egyptian pyramids drank beer at the end of the day. Those laborers were not women."

"So doing as the Egyptian laborer did when he built the pyramids makes me look sexy. Okay. Then explain that look you gave me when I ordered my beer."

"Heineken?" he said. "Nadia Tesla drinking the most popular beer in the world? Where's the iconoclast? Where's the originality? Are you feeling okay?"

"I'm blending in. Doing what the locals do, you know?"

"You'll never blend in," Simmy said. "You're too intense. Have you had a chance to examine the *matryoshka*?"

The Russian nesting doll had never been far from my mind since he'd given it to me, until today. It had been lurking, right behind whatever was consuming me at any given moment, holding the promise of future revelations and excitement with my favorite client. But once I'd been lifted off the street and my clothes had been removed and I'd been politely told to get the hell out of town, I'd forgotten all about it.

"It's incredibly beautiful, Simmy," I said. "The workmanship ... the design ... and the painting ..."

"Meaning I've gotten the better of you so far, and you've discovered none of the meaning I told you they hold." A look of delight spread on his face as though I'd made his day.

"You seem pleased about that," I said.

"Do I? A friend of mine recently introduced me to this new concept called delayed gratification. Any time I get to practice it, I feel as though I'm evolving."

I shifted in my seat. "A friend, huh? I thought you didn't have any friends."

"I didn't. Now, I'm not so sure. New horizons, as we discussed last time, you know?"

"You're full of surprises," I said. "I'll give you that."

"Keep studying the matryoshka," Simmy said. "Individually, and collectively. Break it apart so you can see each doll. Weigh their individual consciences. Each doll has its own personality. To understand the Russian nesting doll is to the key to understanding a Russian man, which is the key to understanding life."

"Ha." I suppressed a belly laugh. "The key to understanding life?"

Simmy remained stoic. "That is correct."

"Okay, then, boss, I'll get right on that," I said. De Vroom's assertion that he was certain a Russian man had killed Iskra echoed in my ears. "I do want to understand the Russian man. Speaking of which, have you made any progress on the political front?"

Simmy played with his glass. "He hasn't returned my call yet. Not that this is entirely unusual. He's been traveling throughout Europe on diplomatic matters so obviously he's busy."

Simmy looked around as though making sure no one had crept up within earshot.

"You always do that," I said.

"What do I do?"

"Get paranoid when you're talking about Putler, even when we're in Amsterdam, or New York City, for that matter."

Simmy repeated the exercise. I got the sense that this was an instinct that he couldn't control.

"It pays to be paranoid," he said. "Perhaps I'm wrong about the reason he hasn't returned my call. Perhaps I should be concerned there might be poison in my food."

"As in, tonight?" I said.

"As in every night."

I waited for him to crack a smile or give me some sign he was joking but he simply sat there looking serious. As the pause in our conversation lengthened, my expression must have betrayed my concern.

Finally, he chuckled. "Relax, I'm kidding. Like I said, this isn't unusual. I'm sure we'll talk soon. In fact, I wouldn't be surprised if he summoned me for a face-to-face in Europe any day." Then he turned philosophical. "But if it ever got to that point, poison would be the primary concern."

"You're serious now."

"It was the Soviet way and the current ways are anchored in the Soviet ways. In 2006, a politician by the name of Anatoly Sobchak was killed in Russia when he breathed in a poison that had been sprayed onto a light bulb. He turned the lights on, the electricity heated the bulb and vaporized the poison. Later in 2006, an FSB whistle-blower named Alexander Litvinenko was poisoned in London. The assassin put polonium in his teapot. That was a stupid move because polonium is radioactive, so the police were able to trace it and find the assassin's name. He later became a member of Russian parliament, by the way. And back in 1959, there was the murder of the famous Ukrainian politician, Stepan Bandera. Death by cyanide poisoning. Delivered by a poison atomizer mist gun. Basically, the assassin sprayed cyanide in Bandera's face, and got the hell out of there before he breathed some himself."

"To most Americans, that would sound like the stuff of fiction," I said.

"Well, we Russians know better. There's actually a rumor that someone tried to kill Putler that way."

"Really?" I said. "When?"

"Within the last six months. They say that's why he's become so cautious, rarely appearing in public. That may be one of the reasons I haven't heard from him. Who knows? Supposedly it was an old-school coup attempt by an assassin unknown using the old-school poison mist gun they used to kill Bandera. The rumor is Putler is so sharp, so focused, and so suspicious that he saw it happening. And he's so physically fit, so quick for his age, he darted out of harm's way. His secretary wasn't so lucky. She died almost instantly. But not instantly, you know? There was just enough lag for her to realize what was happening to her before she went."

Simmy shook his head, looking genuinely horrified.

"That's terrible," I said, picturing the woman struggling for her last breath.

"It's common knowledge in our circles in Russia. When you see a suspicious death, if there's a bodyguard or secretary lying on the ground, too, you can bet it was poison."

"No wonder Putler's so careful," I said. "No wonder he's the man he is."

"You're wrong."

"How am I wrong? You yourself just said he's paranoid—"

"Putler's not a man," Simmy said.

"Excuse me?"

"He's not a single man. He's whatever he needs to be to get what he wants. He's not one man, he's not two men. He's a collection of personalities, any of which he can use to pursue his personal agenda. He's a statesman, a sportsman, a father, a liar and a thug, but above all else, at the very core of the man is an insecure boy."

I thought of my father, brother and deceased husband.

"I've known a few of those," I said.

"He was born in Leningrad - now St. Petersburg –after the siege of World War II. The city was in ruins. He grew up in poverty and hopelessness, in the courtyards surrounding the apartment buildings, where drinking, smoking and fistfights were the norm. He was short and skinny but he never backed down in a fight, and even though he was the runt of the litter he was the enforcer among his group of friends. He had a vicious temper but what made him so effective as a leader among children, what made him so dangerous, was that he could control it.

"He was the type of kid who would see a friend getting abused, walk over, help break it up, and smooth things over. Then, after a few hours passed and all seemed to be forgotten, he'd come back, find the thug that beat his friend, and hurt him.

He was calculating that way. He would wait until the field was tilted in his favor before he got his vengeance.

"When Valery joined the KGB after university it was overstaffed and the Soviet Union was falling apart. He ended up stationed in Berlin cutting newspaper articles and filing useless reports. But he stayed true to himself. He controlled his temper and he didn't make enemies. And he let his greatest attribute of all get him promoted."

"Which was?"

"He didn't offend anyone. He didn't intimidate anyone. He appeared accessible, average, and totally malleable. He was polite. He remembered the birthday of the wives of men senior to him. If a man fell out of favor, and he was a friend, Putler didn't abandon him. He didn't shun him like a disease the way most KGB officers did. At least not right away. That's why his predecessor's inner circle chose him to be Prime Minister. To people in the field, Putler seemed average, but to the leaders of the country he appeared amazing. He had redeeming qualities they didn't see in themselves. He even looked different. He was fit and wore stylish European suits. He wasn't fat and bloated like most Russian politicians."

"And now the west considers him the embodiment of evil," I said.

"The west sees Valery as the embodiment of evil because that's exactly how he wants the west to see him."

"And he wants to be perceived as the root of all evil in the west because …"

"Because it makes him the most popular man in Russia. It's the world against Russia. Russia against the world. Russians crave a return to their former imperialist ways because it gives them a source of joy. It gives them something to believe in. Valery embodies that hope."

"But they need something to believe in because he runs a repressive regime," I said. "There's no political, economic, or personal freedom."

"But in his mind, if it weren't him, some other man would be doing the exact same thing. He knows no other form of government. And to him and his ilk, America and the west are hypocrisies. You have social problems. Inequality of income, persecuted minorities. Your system of governing creates far from perfect results."

"We elect our senators and representatives, our governors and our mayors. Our president doesn't appoint them to suit his needs. I'll stick with our system of government, thank you very much. There's a reason Russian oligarchs park most of their money in London, isn't there?"

He shrugged. I detected uncertainty beneath his bravado. It was intangible and might have been invisible to anyone who hadn't spent a certain amount of time with him. But it was there, in his heart and soul. I could feel it.

I thought of Romanov and his thesis yet again, and wondered if this insecurity and his quest to find Iskra's murderer could be related.

"Simmy," I said, after we sipped our drinks, "you hired me to look into Iskra's death because Maria Romanova is a close friend of yours."

"Was a close friend. Is an old friend. Semantics, yes?"

"How did that come about? Did you learn of Iskra's death and contact Maria, or did she call asking for help?"

Simmy looked confused.

"Humor me," I said. "There's a reason I'm asking."

"I heard about it through normal channels. The expat community is a small one, where my social circle is concerned. Then I called Maria and spoke to her – and George – and offered to help."

"Offered?"

"Yes," Simmy said. "Good point. George wasn't too keen on getting any assistance from me but I insisted anyways."

"And this is the only reason you hired me?"

Simmy frowned. "I don't understand. What other possible reason could there be?"

"I don't know. That's what I'm trying to find out."

"Where is this coming from? Why are you asking me this question?"

"The odds are high that a Russian national killed Iskra. I'm just trying——"

"Why do you say this?" Simmy said. "Do you know something? Do you have new information?"

"Call it instinct," I said, "based on some new interviews I had today."

"With whom did you have these interviews?"

I motioned with my hands for him to calm down. "Let me do my job. When I have tangible news, you'll be the first person I call. But it's important that I know you're being completely honest with me."

Simmy sat back in his chair and reflected on my question for a brief moment.

"I hired you as a favor for an old friend. Beyond that, if I'm keeping anything secret from you," he said, his voice back to the soft and supple one with which he'd started the evening, "the matryoshka will inform you."

CHAPTER 21

When I got back to the hotel, I changed into sweatpants and a t-shirt, and snagged a Diet Coke from the minibar, except they don't call it Diet Coke in most of Europe. They call it Coca-Coca Light because most Europeans have never heard of a "diet" food. And yet America is the one with the obesity problem. Is there any doubt the two are related?

After a sip of my artificially flavored soft drink, I put the *matryoshka* and a box of chocolates on my bed and propped myself up with a pillow. Then I took apart Simmy's gift and assembled each of the seven nesting dolls individually. Afterwards, I arranged them in a row by size.

I popped a caramel into my mouth and studied them. Simmy was a thoughtful man who enjoyed musing philosophically, but his observations about the nesting dolls sounded scripted. A wooden object didn't have a conscience. And once you coupled the proper tops and bottoms and assembled the seven figurines, the dolls held no remaining mysteries. Or did they?

It was Simmy's choice of words that made me think there was more to the dolls than met the eye. Why did he tell me to weigh their individual consciences? Was that his way to suggest that the relative weights of the individual dolls offered a clue to the supposed knowledge they contained? Or was I thinking too much?

I held each pair of dolls of successive heights in my hands. The weights seemed proportionate to the dolls' sizes. If there were something hidden inside the wood that comprised one of the figurines, surely I would have sensed the extra weight in my hands. Unless the object in question was very light, I thought.

There was only one way to find out for certain.

I called room service and ordered some herbal tea. I also asked the staff to send up a food scale. I told them I'd bought some snacks and needed to be precise with my food consumption. I doubt it was the strangest request they'd ever encountered.

Half an hour later, the food and the scale arrived. I tipped the delivery man ten euro to show my appreciation for the scale and he seemed thrilled. After he left, I put the scale and the nesting dolls on my desk.

I assigned each doll a number from one to seven, starting with the largest and ending with the smallest. I used the paper-thin measuring tape in my travel-size sewing kit to estimate the length, width and depth of each doll. Then I weighed them individually, and calculated a weight per cubic inch ratio for each one. When I was finished, I had my answer.

Six of the dolls produced ratios close to the average. One of them, however, was an outlier. Doll number two, the second largest nesting doll, weighed more for its size than the others. I'd been unable to detect this manually because doll number one was so much larger than number two that the smaller one still felt light in my hands. But my statistical analysis had proven that number two should have weighed even less.

There were only two possible explanations for this. Either the craftsman had used a different kind of wood for the second doll, or there was a foreign object inside it. I doubted the craftsman had used different wood for one of the dolls. I suspected the raw material was machine-cut from one batch. The craft was in the painting.

That suggested there really was something else inside doll number two. I picked it up and caressed it the way Simmy had suggested.

As I studied its construction, I reflected on how much Simmy trusted me. I couldn't shake the notion that such trust was the manifestation of grand affection. He'd shared information with me about his relationship with Valery Putler. These were the type of intimate details that could get a man in serious trouble. Had a man ever displayed such faith in me and my discretion? Had I ever mattered that much to any person? My parents had given me life and raised me, but I was their child and that was different. Beyond the parental link, my mother and father had remained emotionally detached with me. I'd never felt as though I'd truly known them. I'd known my brother when I was a child and he was my hero, but we'd grown apart as we'd matured. And as for my ex-husband …

I opened doll number two and ran my fingers along the interior of the top and bottom pieces. The sides appeared too thin to hide any object. The rounded top was equally fine, but the base had a little extra wood to it, probably for ballast. If I were an artist instructed to hide something within the doll, I would focus on its lower half. The bottom was painted pink – the color of borsch preferred by Russians as opposed to Ukrainians, with sour cream added. Meticulous sanding, some fine glue, and the bold-colored paint could hide an opening created to sneak a foreign object inside.

My next course of action displeased me, for although the doll was an inanimate thing, I didn't relish the surgery I needed to perform. The *matryoshka* was a gift from Simmy and I hated the thought of destroying it. But even more than that, Simmy's comment had imbued the damn thing with a certain mysticism. I hoped I wasn't provoking some sort of curse by damaging it. Not that I believed in curses per say, but as a policy, I avoided encouraging negative superstitions on the off-chance there was actually some substance to them.

I picked up the hotel phone again. This time I called housekeeping and requested a small handsaw. Anything that could cut wood with some precision, I said. I told them one of the handles on my luggage had come undone and rather than leave it dangling during my trip I wanted to cut it off. Did they have a Swiss army knife, preferably one of the Huntsman variety, that came with a saw and a knife? My years as Ukrainian girl scout had informed me on the subject.

This time I suspected my request was a bit more eccentric. Nevertheless, fifteen minutes later a man in plain clothes arrived with a vintage Dutch army knife. It had an olive handle and looked as though it had survived a war. I tipped him ten euro, too, and promised to call housekeeping as soon as I was done.

Then I sawed through the bottom of doll number two. The tool's saw was a crude device, built to rip and cut with certainty, not precision. It had some rust but the blade tore through the balsa wood with a modest amount of pressure. Half an inch in, I hit something solid. I pulled the blade out. Whatever I'd hit was black in color and resistant to sawing. I cut around it until the bottom of the doll fell off. Then I plucked the black object from within.

It was rectangular in shape, one inch by one and half inches in length and width, and no more than a quarter inch in thickness. The saw had left a few scrapes. I suspected it was a box built to protect something but there was no hinge or indication of how one might open it. The box seemed a little heavier than the plastic warranted. I shook it and listened, but didn't hear anything move inside.

I reached for my box of caramels. Mouth full of chocolate, I tried to think of other plastic devices. The remote control to some of the latest gizmos came to mind. They were relatively small and simple in design. The backs came off for battery replacement but they weren't always easy to remove. One had to press down in the appropriate place and then push to slide the cover off …

I succeeded on my third try.

One side of the box slid out lengthwise.

A silver key shimmered inside.

I pulled it out. It had notches on both sides and looked brand new. There was no lettering on it. No indication whatsoever of what it might open.

Simmy's words echoed in my head.

"To understand the Russian nesting doll is to the key to understanding a Russian man, which is the key to understanding life."

I'd laughed when I'd heard it but I wasn't laughing now. Perhaps what Simmy really meant was that there was a key inside one of the nesting dolls, and only with that key would I, Nadia Tesla, understand him, Simeon Simeonovich. And only if I understood him would I understand my life and the truth about myself.

I didn't know how a key could possibly help me understand him, or how understanding him would help me comprehend my own life, but I was certain that I had to find out, no matter what the risk to life and limb, just as surely as I knew that finding Iskra's killer was the prerequisite to discovering the answer.

CHAPTER 22

The next morning I worked out at the hotel gym, showered, and went to the dining room for breakfast. I stuck to my spinach and egg white omelet and tried to avoid the pastry table but it didn't work. Yesterday's encounter with the thugs had finally tilted the chemical imbalance in my brain past the point of endurance. I inhaled the first chocolate croissant and savored the sublime chocolate filling. It wasn't saturated with sugar the way it might have been in many American bakeries. I was reaching for the other one I'd added to my plate when I got the shock of the morning.

Maria Romanova stood in front of my table, a crimson folio the size of a tablet computer in her hands.

"Good morning," I said.

I stood up as soon as I saw her. It was an act of respect – she was my elder – and gratitude, because I knew right away that she'd come bearing some sort of information. Why else would she be at my hotel? But more telling was her appearance. She looked even more dreadful than when I'd first met her, as though someone or something were literally sucking the life out of her.

She wanted to tell me something. She needed to tell me something, I thought.

"You're still here," she said.

I smiled. "Where else would I be?"

She hesitated. "I thought you might have gone back home."

"Why would you think that?"

"I didn't know when you were leaving. I don't think we ever discussed that, did we?"

"No," I said. "You're right. We didn't."

I asked her to sit down, my heart pounding with the possibility that somehow Maria Romanova knew about my abduction yesterday, and the threat I'd received. And if she was aware of it, she'd still come to visit me just in case I was still here. Perhaps she'd assumed I'd made flight reservations yesterday for an early departure this morning.

"Coffee or tea?" I said, motioning for a waiter to come over. "And you must eat something. It's a buffet but they can make you an omelet if you like."

She settled for white toast with raspberry jam and some tea. This time she spread the jam on the bread as opposed to adding a dollop to her tea. That was a most promising development, I thought.

"This is a pleasant surprise," I said.

"It is," she said, before sipping her tea. "And speaking of surprises, I have one for you."

She unzipped the folio. Instead of a tablet computer, it held a picture frame. Maria pulled the frame out, bottom side up, and handed it to me without turning it over.

"I don't think you ever saw this picture," she said. "It's a recent one. It was in my bedroom. I thought you might like to see it."

I held my breath as I flipped the frame to study the picture but what I saw quickly doused my enthusiasm. It was just another photo of the family and their surrogate son, Sasha, posing at an outdoor concert, a throng of people between them and the bandstand in the distance. It was a relatively recent shot, I was sure, because Iskra was smiling. These were among her final days, I thought – the Sarah Dumont days, I'd come to call them, knowing her lover was the source of the joy in her expression. In that regard and all others, the picture was the same as the ones I'd seen in her home. The spectators surrounding the family had their backs to the camera, which had a shallow depth of focus that added to the photo's appeal. Other than the Romanovs, everyone and everything else was pretty much out of focus.

"Nice," I said. "When was this taken?"

"The weekend before she died. It's the last picture I have of my girl," Maria said.

I continued to study it to no benefit. When I glanced at Maria, she was spooning some jam into her tea. I suspected my hopes and fantasies had gotten the better of me. As the jam slip off her spoon into the steaming tea, any optimism I had that she'd arrived informed about my plight and armed with valuable information disappeared with it.

I touched the edge of frame with the tips of my fingertips as though it were a priceless object.

"She was very lovely, Iskra was," I said, and pushed the picture across the table back to her mother.

Maria mixed the jam into her tea, stared randomly into space, then turned her attention to me and looked completely lucid. "That she was."

"Is there anything you remember about her final days that you didn't have a chance to tell me about when we first me? Anything that struck you as noteworthy upon further reflection?"

She thought about it for a moment, then shook her head and resumed drinking her tea.

The visit was the exact opposite of what I though it would be when she'd arrived. I sympathized with her and considered it a matter of honor to provide her with some comfort, especially given she'd come to see me of her own volition. But Simmy wasn't paying me to be thoughtful with the victim's mother.

The thought of Simmy brought to mind a second line of questioning, one that was of personal interest to me.

"Maria, may I ask you a question about Simmy?"

She raised her eyebrows. "Simmy?"

"Were you surprised when he called you to offer to help with the case?"

"Not really."

"Why not?" I said.

"Because he has a big heart. And it's just like him to do something like this for an old … an old friend, like me."

"That means you stayed in touch all these years, right? I mean, if it wasn't a surprise, you had to have some contact with him. It's not as though he called you after twenty years and offered his services, is it?"

Maria considered the question, then began counting on her fingers. She seemed to lose track, gave me an apologetic look and repeated the process.

"Twenty-four," she said.

"Twenty-four years?"

She smiled and nodded. "What a guy, huh?"

"So you didn't stay in touch all these years?"

"Of course not. We went our separate ways. He got married, I got married. Once there are spouses, it's very hard to maintain a friendship with someone that you were emotionally intimate with."

"And yet you say weren't surprised when he called? Twenty-four years later?"

Maria considered my question. "I guess you're right, when I think about it from that perspective. But this wasn't a Christmas holiday or a birthday, it was quite the opposite so I thought it was very sweet of him. George didn't care for it, of course – Russian men are very possessive, even of their old wives. And as I said, it was just like Simmy to reach out to someone after all these years."

"I understand," I said. "Was there any other reason he might have reached out? To your knowledge?"

"Another reason?" She appeared baffled by the question. Then she brightened. "Oh, you mean do I think he missed me after all these years?"

"Well ..."

"I'd love to say that I think that's the case, but I'm not that delusional. Not anymore. Twenty years ago? Yes. Ten years ago? Maybe. It takes time to accept the ravages of age, vodka, and a slowing metabolism. Today? No. Give me self-awareness over delusion any day."

I was left speechless, once again uncertain about Maria's state of mind now that she sounded more in control of her faculties than most people I knew. I thought of myself yesterday, trying to remain in control of my thoughts while my assailants stripped my clothes from my body.

My eyes drifted to the picture she'd brought. I studied it again.

"Have you seen Sasha recently?" I said.

"He calls all the time to see how I am."

"That's nice."

"As a matter-of-fact he called yesterday," Maria said. "Said he was going away for a couple of nights to take his mind off things. Who can blame him? The poor boy, he loved Iskra so much. He called because he wanted to know if there was anything he could do for me. He's hopeless, that Sasha, but he's a good soul."

She took a quick sip of tea.

"I've taken enough of your time. I should be going," she said, and reached into her bag for her wallet

"No, no," I said. "Please. It's my pleasure."

Maria thanked me and stood up. "I just wanted you to see this picture." She took her folio but instead of putting the frame back inside, she slid it toward me. "You should keep it. I think it's important ... it's important that you keep it."

She spoke slowly, emphatically but most noteworthy was the magnitude of pain in her expression. I slid the picture toward myself, inspired by the resurrection of the possibility that it held a clue regarding Iskra's murder, as did the inconsolable look in Maria's face. She really had needed to tell me something, I realized, and she was doing so now.

My eyes fell on the young man in the photo once again.

"Where did you say Sasha was going?" I said.

Her eyes widened for no more than a split second, but it was enough to let me know that I was asking the right question.

"Bruges," she said.

When the word escaped her lips, she closed her eyes and took a barely audible breath, the kind that sounded like relief.

She turned and left, but by then my mind was focused on Sasha's choice of vacation destinations and his image in the picture. I studied him repeatedly. Then I looked at the Romanov family individually, and returned my attention to Sasha.

Then the truth hit me. The clue was right there in front of me all along from the moment Maria Romanova had handed me the picture, but I'd been preoccupied by the faces to see what really mattered.

I whipped out my cell phone and found Simmy's private number. My means of stabilizing my mobile communications device echoed my discovery in the photograph.

It was all in the wrist.

CHAPTER 23

Simmy picked up on the third ring.

"I need your help and I need it now," I said.

He didn't answer right away and I knew why. I hadn't started the conversation by trying to be clever. I was purposefully blunt and direct. Based on our experiences in Siberia tracking my cousin, I knew he'd read me correctly.

"I'm listening," he said.

"I need to get to Bruges now. I need someone serious to go with me. I'm not one hundred percent sure but I think it's a matter of life and death."

"Whose life and death?"

"The girl. Iskra's lover. Sarah Dumont."

This time there was a slightly longer pause.

"I'll drive you myself," he said. "No bodyguards. Just you and me. We'll be less conspicuous."

I'd never seen Simmy drive a car let alone travel without his bodyguards. "You know how to drive a car?"

He sighed. "I've driven in the 24 Hour Le Mans three times under a different name. In case you don't know, that's the most prestigious endurance race in the world."

"That's incredible ... Wait, why under a different name?"

"To hide the results ... Because I'm no good at it and I don't want my weaknesses to give confidence to my adversaries ... To protect my business and my ego ... To serve my vanity as in all matters."

His confession was so obviously real and true, no further words were needed.

"Where am I picking you up?" he said.

"At my hotel," I said. "And I have another request, Simmy. But I'm hesitant because I don't want to offend you."

"When you put it like that, there's not much chance I'll say no, is there?"

"Bring the bodyguards," I said, and hung up.

I wanted the bodyguards to accompany us because I could smell his testosterone over the phone. There was no reason to worry about being conspicuous. We were going to one and only one house and it was secluded. And I didn't need Simmy to be my hero. I wanted us to survive the trip.

Afterwards, I called Sarah Dumont. She answered on the second ring. I identified myself and she sounded understandably surprised to hear from me.

We exchanged hellos.

"I don't want to alarm you." I said, "but I think the person who killed Iskra is coming to Bruges."

"You know who killed her?" she said.

"Not for certain. But I think I do."

She chuckled like a supervisor criticizing an overly confident subordinate. "You think you do?"

"Thinking usually precedes certainty. Yes, I think I do, and when I have this kind of conviction, I'm usually right. If I'm right, the killer is a very resourceful and dangerous person."

"And you think the killer's coming here? For what reason?"

I stayed quiet, knowing she'd answer her own question.

"To kill me, too?"

I remained mute.

"No one would dare try to kill me," she said.

Sarah Dumont had seemed a bit entitled and aloof when I'd met her, but never this arrogant or delusional.

"Why wouldn't anyone dare to kill you?" I said.

"Because … because I have the best security service in Amsterdam." She sounded as though she'd searched for a convenient answer and found one at the last second.

"Are your men there now?" I said.

"Of course they're here. If they weren't here, they wouldn't be the best service in Amsterdam, would they?"

"How many are there? Is it just the two men at the gate? Or is there a third one?"

She chuckled again. "Talking to you is like talking to my mirror. You're a bit of a control freak, aren't you? Now, are you going to answer my question or should I just hang up?"

I backtracked, remembered her question, and told her why I thought Iskra's killer was going to try to kill her. In doing so, I identified the killer.

She didn't chuckle this time. "You cannot be serious."

"If talking to me is like talking to a mirror, do I even need to answer that?"

She considered my comment. "And you think he's coming here today?"

"He may already be there. I think you should consider calling the police—"

"No police."

Her firmness suggested she had other reasons she didn't want the police involved. I wondered what they were.

"I won't be intimidated on my own property," she said. "I worked too hard for it. My father worked too hard for it. I have my security guards. There's two of them. They're trained. Highly trained. I'll tell them what you told me."

I told her I was on my way to Bruges and that I'd call when I got there. In the meantime, I asked her to call me if any visitors arrived, even if they were people she knew. She ended the call without promising to do so.

Simmy and his bodyguards met me in front of my hotel an hour later at 11:30 a.m. They came in two Mercedes Benz vehicles. One was the conservative-looking black sedan that I'd found waiting for me outside of jail. The other was a steroid-injected beast in gunmetal gray. The wheels filled their wells, the front bumper looked ravenous, and steam poured from four tail pipes in the rear.

Simmy arrived driving the latter.

"And you wanted to be less conspicuous?" I said.

"Don't be ridiculous," Simmy said. "This is a masquerade. A sports car disguised as a sedan. If I wasn't behind the wheel, you wouldn't have looked twice at this car."

"You're right about that."

"Not an automobile enthusiast? How can that be when you drive that old 911?"

"I wasn't talking about the car. I meant you're right. This is a masquerade. It's about a person pretending to be one thing but actually being another."

I tried to enter Sarah Dumont's address into Simmy's navigation system, but her home had been built after the map in his system had been designed. Instead, I found the address for the City Center under tourist sites, entered it, and we took off for Bruges.

"Why are you driving yourself?" I said.

"Because I want to prove that I can still do the small things. That I can be a hands-on kind-of guy. Is it working?"

"You bet," I said.

We stopped once to get gas, use the restrooms and buy food. I chose a protein bar, the bodyguards opted for ham and cheese sandwiches, and Simmy stuck with coffee. We hustled through our stop with a minimum of conversation and were back on the road in less than fifteen minutes. I called Sarah Dumont from the car after we left the rest stop. She'd warned the guards to be careful, told me to stop being paranoid, and once again hung up on me. We arrived in Bruges' City Center in the early afternoon, covering the entire one hundred and fifty miles in less than three hours.

I'd taken the taxi to Sarah Dumont's house twice, so I thought I'd have no problem navigating us to her house.

I was wrong.

I made two blunders, including sending us down a narrow one-way street. I could feel Simmy tense when he had to come to a stop, call his boys on the mobile phone, and tell them to back-up. There wasn't enough room to execute a K-turn. He took a few audible breaths as though to calm himself down, but sounded serene as spring.

"What looks like a disaster is actually an opportunity," he said, as he gunned the engine in reverse.

"It is?" I said.

"Certainly. It's an opportunity for us to prove to ourselves that we're mentally strong, that we're invulnerable, and that we're fully composed and prepared to capture this killer."

I glanced at him twice to make sure some spirit hadn't inhabited his body. "We are?"

"I know you're just having fun with me when you say that. After all, you're the warrior and I'm the spoiled rich man. Am I right?"

Once he'd backed out of the alley, he whipped the car around and passed the bodyguards.

I corrected my mistakes and got us to the familiar fork in the road.

"That way," I said, pointing up the hill.

I dialed Sarah Dumont's number to let her know we were a mile away. My call rolled over to voice mail. As I listened to her recorded message telling me to be sure I really needed to talk to her and only then to leave my name, number and a brief message, I suspected she'd recognized my digits and simply didn't want to speak to me anymore.

But when the gate came into view I feared otherwise. I feared otherwise because there was no one in sight.

"Where are the guards?" Simmy said. "You said there'd be guards."

"Maybe one of them is in the guardhouse. It's kind of big. There might be a bathroom in there."

Simmy called the bodyguards and barked some clipped instructions that consisted of the kind of shorthand people who work closely develop over time. I didn't fully comprehend it all, but I knew they were going to check the guardhouse.

Simmy pulled up to the gate. The bodyguards turned their car around and backed-up with their trunk facing the house.

"What are they doing?" I said.

"Preparing for a quick departure, just in case. This way we're ready to go in either direction. Just like American politics. In Russia it would be much easier. If you want to live, there is only one direction to go and that is forward. Outside of Russia, you can never be sure. Wait in the car."

He exited the vehicle. I flung the door open and followed him to the guardhouse. Simmy stopped and glared at me but knew better than to waste his energy trying to stop me.

The forest obscured the sunlight from above. The glass house stood beyond the gate surrounded by trees. Both of Sarah Dumont's cars were parked in front of the entrance in the same places, except their locations were reversed from the previous night. There was no sign of life. The entire property appeared to be taking a nap.

Inside the guardhouse, a tall chair faced the window with a view of the road. The chair was empty. A computer rested on a narrow desktop between the chair and the window. The monitor displayed an article written in Dutch and included a picture of two soccer players vying for the ball. Vanilla crème cookies spilled from an open bag onto the desk. Steam rose from a mug of coffee. Someone had been here a moment ago, I thought, but I didn't share my observation with anyone for fear of making any unnecessary noise.

A door led to a back room. I could tell from the structure's exterior dimensions that the space was a small one, no bigger than a pantry or a small bathroom.

Simmy looked beyond me and nodded.

I turned. The bodyguards had arrived. One stood on my heels hulking over me like a giant human Pez dispenser ready to gobble me up. A glint of metal caught my eyes. I looked down and saw the stainless steel gun in his hand. The other bodyguard stood outside, scanning the house and the road. He held an assault rifle. It looked slick, terrifying and seductive.

It was when I turned back that I got the biggest shock of all.

Simmy was knocking on the door to the back room. His knock sounded like banging on a hollow drum because the door appeared to be a cheap empty shell. What astonished me was that his fingers were wrapped around his own gun.

No one answered. He glanced at me as he waited.

"You have a gun?" I said.

He answered me by holding my eyes for an extra second. Then he knocked once more, waited for a count of three, and grabbed the doorknob.

It rattled but didn't turn completely. It was locked.

Simmy nodded at the bodyguard closest to him again. Then he stepped back toward me and let the bodyguard slide past us.

I leaned into his ear. "Why do you have a gun?"

He gave me a puzzled look. "Because I'm prepared. Why don't you have one?"

"Because I don't want to shoot myself."

He nodded. "I was with the military police in the army. You weren't. With my men and me at your disposal your arsenal is complete. All is as it should be."

The bodyguard rammed the door with his shoulder. The door frame cracked. He rammed it twice more.

The door caved in. The bodyguard stood in the doorway obscuring the interior of the room. Simmy stepped up beside him and looked inside.

"Son-of-a-bitch," he said, in a clipped and breathless manner.

The bodyguard thrust his gun into his left hand and stepped further into the room. When he bent over to check for pulses, Sarah Dumont's guards were revealed.

They were both dead.

CHAPTER 24

The crimson wall in Iskra's bedroom had transfixed me with its gruesome depiction of the evil that one human being could perpetrate against another. The guards' bodies had an entirely different effect on me. They made my nerves stand on edge with the knowledge that all our lives, in fact, were in danger. But they also boosted my confidence. The murder of these men, seemingly innocents in this matter, was tragic collateral damage. And yet it proved my theory about the killer to be correct and, as a result, galvanized my senses.

While the bodyguards and Simmy exchanged words, I snuck in from behind them. The carcass of the guards' pet, the wolf who had attacked me, lay beside their bodies. One guard had been killed by a shot to the forehead. The other had been shot twice in the chest before also being shot in the head. Perhaps the killer had surprised them at the gate, shot the first guard in the head, then fired two rounds into the other guard's chest before the man could square his weapon. Then he'd finished him off with the shot to the forehead. The wolf had probably been tethered to his post and never had a chance.

The sight of the dead animal bothered me as much or more than the sight of the human corpses. Maybe that was wrong, but there was no denying its truth.

I grabbed Simmy by the arm. "We have to get in there now, " I said. "What did your bodyguards do before they became bodyguards?"

"They dealt with situations like this," Simmy said. "That is why you're going to wait here and let us do what's necessary."

"Us? You mean them."

Simmy glared at me. "You will stay here."

"Okay, boss. You're the client. Whatever you say."

Simmy conferred with the bodyguards. After a thirty second discussion where the bodyguards did most of the talking, one of the guards brought four vests from the trunk of the black Mercedes. Each of us put one on. Mine needed strap adjustments to fit my smaller frame and still felt too big.

Then the bodyguard with the assault rifle raced past the gate. He used the tree line as cover and disappeared from sight.

Less than a minute later Simmy's phone trilled. The bodyguard had circled the house and gotten the layout. They had another chat. I knew Simmy didn't want to get us all killed and precautions were necessary but precious seconds were ticking away. I finally couldn't take it anymore.

"Simmy," I said.

He raised a finger and nodded at me, as though reassuring me that he, too, was ready to jump out of his skin. Then he hung up and headed for the driver's seat to his Mercedes. I expected the bodyguard to head for the passenger side but he didn't. Instead, he raised the gate and took his position directly behind the car.

I recognized my opportunity, sprinted around him, and got to the passenger front door just as Simmy had one foot in the driver's side.

"What are you ..."

I slid inside and shut the door before he could finish his sentence.

Simmy slipped behind the wheel. He pressed a button on the armrest and the doors locked with the emphatic thump of a bank vault.

"Seat belt," he said.

I shot him a look. "You're suddenly okay with my going?"

"I'm suddenly aware that this is the safest place for you. My man reconned the property. The house is an optical illusion. There's glass in front but the back of the house is a stone fortress. No windows on the lower level. No access to the windows on the second level. The only way to get inside ... " Simmy started the car and the engine came to life. It sounded like rolling thunder wrapped in silk. "Is through the front door."

Simmy wrapped his hands around the wheel. I rushed to snap my seat belt in place. He pressed the throttle. The engine shed its silky overtones and screamed.

My neck snapped back against my headrest. I felt like the arrow that had been sprung from the crossbow. The Mercedes devoured the tarmac between the gate and the house. My stomach shot up my throat.

I barely heard Simmy speaking. "This is the S65 AMG with six hundred thirty horsepower and one thousand newton metres of torque ..."

The front door appeared dead ahead. To its right, the floor-to-ceiling glass wall. The engine unleashed its full fury.

"Simmy, what the fuck ..."

We were supposed to be slowing down, but we weren't.

Simmy raised his voice so I could hear him over the din but his tone remained shockingly composed. "You should know I've had some modifications made."

We would be upon the door in seconds.

"Ballistic stainless steel, Kevlar, Dyneema ..."

"Oh my God ..."

"Fear for the house," he said, "not for your life."

The car veered right toward the glass window. A row of thick hedges provided a lift.

I closed my eyes.

The front of the car vaulted into the air. The engine stopped wailing.

I heard a thunk. A nanosecond of complete and utter silence followed. My body floated downward, as though being pulled to the Earth by its gravitational pull—

The car landed with a thump.

I opened my eyes.

Glass fell to the floor around us. I felt the brakes grab the wheels. The car slowed instantly but kept rolling.

We pulverized a tinted glass coffee table, piled into an uphol-stered recliner and carried it through the living room. The living room opened into the dining room. I spotted the dining room table a second before we crushed it, an oval sheet of glass atop an asymmetric white stand that looked like a designer vault for skate-boarders. Sleek white side chairs scattered like kites in a hurricane. We plowed through a serving table containing a monumental glass vase and burst through the half-wall beyond it.

The Mercedes stopped.

The car came to rest in front of a center island with a white marble countertop. A box of Alpen cereal, a bottle of almond milk, and a bowl with a spoon rested atop it. The stainless steel stove looked like a duplicate of the one I'd used at Sarah Dumont's restaurant.

Simmy managed to open his door just enough to slip out. Mine was pressed against a tabletop with a giant industrial mixer that looked like it had never been used. Someone liked the idea of home-baked cookies, but didn't want to do the work or consume the calories, I thought.

I swung my legs over the car's center console and pushed off with my arms to propel myself into the driver's seat. Knobs and buttons stabbed my hipbone but adrenaline dulled the pain.

The killer was in the house. He'd murdered two bodyguards and a perfectly nice wolf after I'd told Sarah Dumont that they should all be careful.

Simmy stood with his back against the refrigerator, facing the debris in the living area. A hallway that ran perpendicular to the rooms we'd destroyed was the only other way into the kitchen. It opened up around the corner from Simmy.

As I slipped out the driver's side door, I heard footsteps coming from the direction of the living room.

Both bodyguards had their weapons raised. They were stalking their way toward us through the wreckage. One of them had eyes on the kitchen and the corridor. The other was turned the other way, focused on the path in their wake.

I slipped beside Simmy. I'd be lying if I didn't admit I took comfort in the bodyguards' presence. We had numbers. We had arms. The men who were with me were trained. The question was whether Sarah Dumont was still alive or not.

"Nadia?"

A man had spoken my name. When Simmy looked back at me with the same shock I'd just experienced, I knew I wasn't imagining it. I'd only heard that voice once before, but I recognized it nonetheless. I'd been expecting to hear it soon, just not calling out my name.

The voice sounded again. "Nadia? Are you there?" The man spoke Russian. Fear and urgency punctuated his delivery.

I glanced at Simmy, who looked to the bodyguards. They nodded.

"Sasha?" I let my voice carry to make sure he heard me. "Is that you?"

"I want to come out. I want to surrender. Don't shoot."

The bodyguards spread out and took aim at the corridor. They nodded at Simmy.

Simmy whispered in my ear. "Tell him to come out with his hands up in the air, and if he tries anything, two former members of FSB special forces will shoot him dead, no questions asked."

I repeated what Simmy had told me but peppered my delivery with enthusiasm. I had to give the kid credit. I strongly suspected he'd been manipulated into his current situation. Sufficient time had passed since Iskra's murder for him to contemplate what he'd done, and he'd finally come to his senses.

"I'm coming out," Sasha said. "Don't shoot. I'm unarmed."

Uncertain footsteps came our way, heavy boots over a hardwood floor.

Sasha appeared. He wore the trademark blue trousers and a white short sleeve shirt of the Bruges police. Even more surprising was his head. His dreadlocks were gone. In their place, he wore a baseball cap that matched his uniform.

I leaned into Simmy's ear. "It's Sasha——"

A muffled thud interrupted me.

Sasha collapsed to the floor. Blood trickled from a hole in his head and stained the collar of his white shirt.

"Shit," Simmy and I said, almost simultaneously.

I crept around Simmy, but before I could see Sasha's face, I spotted the watch around his wrist.

It was the same Panerai he'd been wearing at the museum, the one the real killer had been wearing in the Romanov family photo.

CHAPTER 25

I slipped back beside Simmy.

The bodyguards had to be careful about an offensive because they not only had to protect themselves, they had to be concerned with Sarah Dumont's whereabouts. This was obvious even to me, the untrained member of our group, and no words needed to be spoken to make it clearer. And yet the clock was ticking, and for all I knew, Sarah Dumont's throat was being slit even as we stood by absorbing Sasha's death.

And then we heard it. A distant moan. Someone trying to scream but unable to fully open her mouth. It came from where Sasha had appeared, from a room down the corridor on the first level.

The bodyguards motioned to each other with their hands. One made a knife with his right hand, aimed it toward the corridor, and then made a V of his second and third fingers and brought it to his eyes. His partner nodded.

They glanced at Simmy, who nodded back at them. Then he turned at a slight angle toward me so that only I could hear him.

"We're going in," he said.

The bodyguards disappeared down the corridor. Simmy started to follow. It made no sense for him to go until his men had dealt with whatever awaited us. And yet I respected him for his courage, just as surely as I wondered about the motivation behind it, and if he had some connection to Sarah Dumont that had escaped me thus far.

As soon as Simmy negotiated the corner, I followed him. *Sometimes it's better to be imprudent than be labeled a coward, especially by oneself.*

The hallways gave access to a series of doors on both sides. I counted five of them. Three on the left, and two on the right.

All the doors were closed.

The bodyguards whipped the first door open. One of them charged inside.

He returned five seconds later.

They flung the second door open. The other one bust into the room.

There was no one inside.

The bodyguards moved on to the third door. And then the fourth. They moved quickly and efficiently and yet the process was interminable.

They got to the last door on the left. Two closets, an office, and a laundry room preceded this room. A bedroom, I thought. Most folks who built a large home these days made sure the ground floor contained a bedroom.

Simmy's men approached the last door. One of them turned the handle. He rushed inside.

He disappeared from sight but I heard him shout.

"Put the knife down, put the knife down."

The second bodyguard followed the first one and barked something similar. By then Simmy was in the doorway and I was on his heels.

George Romanov stood dressed in a policeman's uniform identical to the one Sasha had been wearing. The gun – presumably the one he'd used to shoot Sasha – was stuck in a holster attached to a belt along his waist. He held a knife to Sarah Dumont's throat. She was naked except for the strip of duct tape around her mouth. Her hands were tied behind her back. Both her eyes appeared swollen and a darker shade of red. I saw a mixture of fear and anger in her eyes but she stood tall with a defiant posture and exuded an astonishing sense of composure. What I did not see was the emotion that would have gripped most people at that moment. I did not see any signs of pure, unadulterated terror.

In fact, the man holding the knife appeared more unsettled. He was the one with sweat on his brow, and I understood why. The men who'd run the former Soviet Union and those who ran Russia now were consumed with one thing – themselves. Romanov was not expecting us even though his wife was the one that had given me the clues about his identity and where to find him. She'd known I'd been kidnapped and threatened because she must have overheard her husband giving the order. Obviously, she knew he'd killed their daughter and she'd been unable to live with herself since then.

"There they are," Romanov said. "The ego and the imbecile."

I knew he wasn't talking about the bodyguards, but I didn't know which moniker belonged to Simmy and which one was mine.

Romanov looked at me. "Maybe not such an imbecile after all."

That clarified things.

As Romanov continued talking, I noticed the chalk outline of a body on the bedroom wall. Four narrow holes had been marked neatly, two for the hands and two for the feet. A toolbox rested on the floor beside a stud finer and a drill.

"You seemed so out of your depth at the dead girl's apartment," Romanov said to me, "so determined to prove to the world that you're a strong person, I never thought for a minute you'd be able to see past your own ambitions. But I guess I was wrong."

"You seemed overwhelmed with grief that day at the crime scene. I never would have guessed you were acting."

"I wasn't acting," Romanov said. "Before she became filth, she was my little girl. And that is who I was remembering."

"Filth?" Simmy said, his words laced with disgust. "The dead girl? That dead girl was your daughter, George. What in God's name has happened to you?"

A heavy silence filled the room. It seemed to grow with each passing second, and if someone didn't speak soon, I was certain we'd all be crushed beneath its weight.

"You murdered your own daughter," Simmy said.

Romanov shrugged. "That shows how little you understand and how weak you are. My daughter died a month ago, long before I killed the disgusting *lesbyanka* she'd become. No flesh and blood of mine would ever act in such an immoral way. She'd never engage in that kind of behavior." He pressed the knife harder against Sarah Dumont's throat. "She'd never touch something like this the way she did."

"Speaking of touching," I said. "Those three men you had attack me yesterday..."

Simmy turned to me. "Who attacked you?"

"Who were they?" I said.

"Men for hire. *Our* kind of men," he said, using the literal translation of *Nashi*. "I told them that you were one of us, to treat you with respect."

I got the feeling he expected me to be grateful. Given a different trio might have done far worse to me, he would have had a point if he hadn't been the man who'd ordered my abduction in the first place. Still, strangely, I couldn't help but appreciate his insistence I not be harmed.

"That's neither here nor there," I said. "That's in the past. Here's the present situation. If you hurt Sarah, these men are going to kill you. But if you let her go, you might walk out of here alive."

"I'm going to walk out of here with her," Romanov said. "You're going to get me a robe and give me the keys to that black Mercedes parked by the gate. We're going to drive away and you're not going to follow us or this thing dies."

When Simmy answered, his entire demeanor changed. Gone was his scolding tone and any sound of displeasure. In their place was the voice of the corporate negotiator, the one who held the most leverage over the eventual outcome of the matter at hand and was dictating proceedings.

"I'm afraid I can't let that happen, George. You have two choices. You can be shot where you stand or you can have the keys to the car and leave here unharmed, if you let her go."

"You're saying you'll let me go if I release this filth?"

"That is what I'm saying," Simmy said. "And my word is good."

"Your boys will shoot me as soon as I take the knife away from her throat."

"No they will not."

"What assurances can you possibly give me? And spare me the lies about your word being good."

"It's quite simple. You're going to take the knife away from her throat and put it against mine."

I stared at Simmy in disbelief.

So did Romanov.

"You heard me," Simmy said. "I'm going to trade you. My life, for her life." He raised his hands in the air, placed his gun on the ground and stepped forward.

"Get back," Romanov said.

Sarah Dumont swept Romanov's feet from under him. It was a swift, practiced, and shocking move.

Romanov fell. His right hand continued gripping the knife. His left hand remained wrapped around Sarah Dumont's neck. He pulled her atop him as he tumbled.

Simmy didn't waste a second. Even before Romanov's body hit the floor, he recovered his gun, aimed and fired.

Blood and brain matter flew from Romanov's head. The knife fell from his grip.

Simmy rushed forward and lifted Sarah Dumont from atop him. She fell into his arms and embraced him as though she'd known him her entire life.

After we all regained our composure, I told Simmy I was calling the cops.

He said he wouldn't have it any other way.

We waited for the police and an ambulance to arrive. Sarah Dumont sustained minor injuries. She thanked us both before she was taken to the hospital. She wasn't any more sentimental than she'd been before, but I could tell her appreciation was heartfelt. I used to think that the eyes never lied, but Sasha and Romanov had proven that theory wrong. In Sarah Dumont's case, however, her eyes spoke the truth when she channeled gratitude Simmy's and my way.

The cops took us to the police station and we gave our statements. We stayed there deep into the night, repeating our stories over and over again. I gave them De Vroom's number and told them to call their counterpart in Amsterdam to learn about Iskra's murder and share news of its resolution. I also told them to tell De Vroom that Sarah Dumont had born witness to Romanov's confession to his own daughter's murder.

Eventually, De Vroom asked to speak with me.

"I told you the killer was a Russian," he said.

"When you busted in on Romanov and me in Iskra's apartment," I said, "you knew we were there because you were following him. He was a suspect, wasn't he?"

"Everyone who knew her was a suspect. We knew she was scared of someone, probably someone close to her."

"Why did you warn me that my investigation could be dangerous? It happened after you ran the license plate and found the SUV was registered to Sarah Dumont."

"Yeah," De Vroom said. "I checked with Bruges police. They said she had connections."

"What kind of connections?"

"They didn't give me details. They just said she had juice. I pressed them but they refused to talk about it. Just told me to tread very, very carefully. So I did. And suggested you do the same. Lucky for us you didn't."

Throughout the night, I saw Simmy on his mobile phone time and again. With each successive call, his expression grew less tense, his carriage became more settled. When the cops finally released us, he looked like the man I'd grown fond of over a year ago, a gentleman and a scoundrel, simultaneously contented yet in search of his next quest.

The cops kept the gray Mercedes as evidence in the case. They let us take the black one. As the bodyguards walked over to the parking lot to retrieve it, Simmy and I waited by the station door.

"Why didn't you tell me you were attacked?" he said. "When was this? Where was this? Exactly what did the men look like?"

"Forget it. It was part of the job. They didn't hurt me. They just threatened me. If I can't take care of myself under duress, I shouldn't be taking these kind of cases."

"You should have told me."

I didn't answer him.

"You should have told me just as I should have told you I was having Iskra Romanova's office watched when you arrived."

"Okay," I said. "In the future, we'll be more open with each other. How's that?"

After a purse of the lips, his expression softened as though that had appeased him. "You exceeded all expectations," he said. "I can't thank you enough."

"That may be true but you can certainly try," I said.

His lips curled up a bit, which was another good sign he'd regained his emotional equilibrium.

"The important thing is that Sarah Dumont is safe and it's all over," I said.

"You solved the murder, but it's not quite over for us," Simmy said. "I need you to do one more little thing for me. It is the simplest, smallest favor a man could ask for."

I started to ask him what exactly he wanted me to do but the car arrived and one of the bodyguard got out to open the door. As we slipped into the backseats, I realized this assignment wasn't over from my perspective, either. I wanted to understand why Simmy had been willing to sacrifice himself for Sarah Dumont. I wanted to understand their connection and what it was about this case that I'd been missing from the beginning.

"When we get to Amsterdam, we'll pick up your things at the hotel and head straight for the airport," Simmy said.

"We will?" I said.

Simmy didn't answer. Instead he looked thoughtfully out the window.

"Where are we going?" I said.

"We're taking you home, of course, and making one quick stop along the way."

"And I presume this stop is where you need me to do you this simplest, smallest favor a man could ask for."

Simmy bowed his head in affirmation. "And even though it's the simplest favor imaginable, I'm throwing in a special bonus if you help me. It's something you desire at the current moment more than anything imaginable."

"You're telling me what I desire? This is some serious role reversal, Simmy. What is it?"

"Thai food. I'm having Amsterdam's best – from the Thai House – delivered to my plane."

My mouth watered.

"You know me too well," I said.

CHAPTER 26

We drove from Bruges to Amsterdam, slogged our way through the morning rush hour, and got back to my hotel mid-morning. I dozed in the car to some hypnotic classical music by the Russian composer, Dmitri Shostakovich.

When I woke up, Simmy told me a story that the famous Borodin String Quartet once went to the composer's house to play his String Quarter No. 8 to get some criticism. Shostakovich had written the symphony after being diagnosed with ALS, Lou Gehrig disease. The quartet's performance evoked the composer's inspiration so beautifully that he sat through the performance weeping with his head in his hands. When they were finished, the musicians took their instruments and snuck out of his home without saying or hearing a word.

After I packed and checked out, we drove to the airport and took off on Simmy's Lineage 1000E. It was a penthouse in the sky with five cabin zones, each opulently appointed with furnishing and electronics. My favorite was the master suite, complete with bathroom ensuite and walk-in shower, which Simmy let me use in complete privacy. When I finished dressing and emerged, a Thai feast was waiting for me in the dining room.

The Treachery of Russian Nesting Dolls

Two sultry Russian cabin attendants served us tom yam soup, pad thai, king prawns in coconut curry and lemon leaves, and duck with ginger and black mushrooms. Simmy and I were both famished so we ate in silence. I told myself to enjoy the food and contain my curiosity about this favor he wanted me to do for him, and his connection to Sarah Dumont. It was, in fact, the latter that fascinated me the most. My instincts told me to be careful. This was the kind of revelation best made voluntarily, though a good investigator could always coax a subject into revealing what she wanted to learn.

After we ate our soup and shared the pad thai appetizer, Simmy drank beer from his frosted glass and exhaled with satisfaction.

"Ah, that's good, isn't it?" he said. "Nothing like cold beer to quench a man's thirst. Except, of course, when it's information he's thirsting for."

"Information?" I couldn't believe he was asking of me what I wanted from him. "What do I know that you don't know?"

"How you solved the damn case. Obviously."

I'd been so focused on what I wanted to find out, I'd forgotten all about my client's inevitable curiosity.

"It wasn't one piece of evidence," I said. "It was several of them. They were there all the time, right in front of me. I just needed time to put them in the proper order and see their connections."

"I don't understand."

"The first thing I look for is a catalyst. If I'm investigating a change in a company's fortunes, trying to figure out how it fell into dire straits, I start by finding the catalyst. The catalyst is usually some company, industry or economic event that changes the normal course of business. It might be something legitimate, like competition, or something criminal, like fraud."

"And what was the catalyst for Iskra's death?" Simmy said.

"Her affair with Sarah Dumont. Or, more precisely, her lesbian affair."

"How did you know it wasn't when she became a window girl?"

"Because Iskra had been working a window in *De Wallen* for months before she got so scared of someone she hired the Turk to walk her home at night. The timing of when she hired protection coincided with when Sasha saw Sarah Dumont coming out of her office disguised as a man. Sasha ambushed her in her own apartment, lost his cool, and told her she was a lesbian whore."

"And this put the fear of God into her?"

"No. Sasha, as the Romanovs were fond of saying, 'was Sasha.' He couldn't put the fear of God into a mouse. The only person who could put the fear of God into her was her father. It took only one lunch for me to see he was fueled by hate. And there was nothing and no one he hated more than a homosexual. Well, except maybe for an American ..."

"But," Simmy said, in a tortured voice, "she was his daughter."

"Not in his eyes. Not once she had sexual relations with a woman. You know the statistics about Russian attitudes toward gays. And Romanov's wife, Maria, reminded me of something very important regarding her husband."

"What was that?"

"Once a Chekhist, always a Chekhist. And Chekhists think they're above the law. In fact, not only do they think they're above the law, they think they're above everyone."

Simmy had never been a Chekhist. He had no background in Russian politics or the secret police, but many of his competitors did, and the politicians who greased the gears of his corporate vehicle were lifetime Chekhists. No one more so than his buddy, Valery Putler.

"How did Romanov find out his daughter was having an affair with Sarah Dumont?" Simmy said.

"Sasha told him. He was his lap dog, the son he never had, though hardly the warrior-type he dreamed of. Sasha knew Romanov would be livid. He knew the father would punish the daughter. He wanted Iskra to be punished. Did he know Romanov was going to kill her ? It's possible. Maybe Sasha loved her so much he fell into a blind rage. But my guess is not. Romanov probably lured him under the pretense of giving Iskra a stern lecture, and once his motives became clear it was too late. Sasha would have been too weak to stop Romanov. Too weak physically, way too weak mentally."

"But how did you know Sasha told Romanov? How did you know they were accomplices?"

"The watch," I said. "Sasha told me the Penerai he was wearing belonged to his father, who died about six years ago. But when Maria Romanova showed me a family picture taken a recently, there it was around a man's wrist. But it wasn't Sasha's wrist. It was George Romanov's."

"Romanov gave Sasha the watch. As what," Simmy said. His elbows rested on the table, hands folded in the air. "A gift of thanks? A bribe for his silence? A token of their ever-lasting friendship now that they'd killed the girl they'd loved their whole lives?"

"All of the above."

Simmy continued staring at me without emotion, but I could sense dismay, disgust, and anger emanating from his side of the table. His emotions were to be expected, I thought. He was a father.

We dug into the prawns and the duck. One of the attendants brought a second round of Singha beers. Simmy poured lager into my glass.

"I was impressed with Sarah Dumont," Simmy said. "I thought she handled herself admirably. What did you think?"

There it was. My opportunity had arrived.

"I don't think she handled herself admirably," I said.

Simmy's eyebrows shot up.

"She handled herself beyond admirably. She was the leg-sweeping, ice-in-her-veins, 'I'll settle the argument, bitch-goddess of the afternoon. Are you kidding me?"

Simmy didn't react to my description. He was back to hiding his emotions, I thought. In the case of Sarah Dumont, that meant there were emotions to hide. A flicker of pride in his eyes increased my suspicion.

"She's clearly had training in self-defense," Simmy said. "A successful young woman on her own, you have to admire her for learning how to take care of herself."

"Is that a guess, or is this something you know for a fact?"

Simmy frowned. "That she's successful and on her own?"

"No. That she's had training in self-defense."

I stared Simmy in the eye, looking for a tell as I waited for his answer. But he gave me neither. Instead, he sipped his beer and ignored my question. I'd done the math in my head a thousand time already. If Simmy was forty-six and Sarah Dumont was twenty-four, he could be her father from a prior relationship. But they could just as easily have been lovers whose paths had crossed at some philanthropic or artistic venue.

"She said some interesting things to me earlier," I said.

"Did she?" Simmy said.

"When I called to tell her that her life was in danger, she said that no one would dare try to kill her."

"Hmm. That's a strange thing to say," he said. "Maybe you heard her wrong."

"I don't think so."

"Maybe she meant to say that no one had a reason to kill her."

"And she said she didn't want the police involved. She said it emphatically."

"Probably a matter of privacy, especially given that nightmare she lived through in Amsterdam. The home invasion. I'm sure she's had enough attention and police to last a lifetime."

Simmy was full of crap. I knew it now, as surely as I knew I'd just lost my appetite for duck, prawns, and carnal knowledge. The questions came to me quickly. I could sense myself going into beast-mode. I was about to interrogate my client. In a minute he would tell me the truth or be revealed to be a no-good, lying Russian dog-of-a-billionaire. It would be the latter, naturally. All men were deceitful shits, why should this one be any different?

"Speaking of getting enough attention," I said, "I sure got your attention when I told you that the murderer's next target was Sarah Dumont."

"And what did you expect? It's not every day a man is told a murder is about to be committed."

"I got the distinct impression the target's identity made all the difference in the world to you."

Simmy hesitated, as though trying to recall our conversation. "Why do you think that? I don't remember saying anything that would give you that impression."

"It's not what you said, Simmy. It's what you didn't say."

He sighed, his first sign of irritation since we'd arrived. "What didn't I say?"

"You didn't say anything. There was dead silence on the line. It was one of those moments were you knew the person on the other end of the line had just had a 'holy shit' moment."

"Fair enough. But be realistic. Your friend calls and speaks of murder ... a man may need a moment to compose himself."

"And there was the proposed trade," I said, "where you offered yourself as a hostage to Romanov in exchange for Sarah."

Simmy remained mute.

"Why would you be so concerned about a stranger?" I said. "The answer is, of course, you wouldn't be. That, in turns, means she isn't a stranger. Sarah Dumont is someone you know. You confirmed that about ninety seconds ago when you said she'd lived through that nightmare in Amsterdam."

He continued staring at me without betraying his emotions.

"I never told you Sarah Dumont had lived through a home invasion, Simmy."

He took a deep breath. When he exhaled, he relaxed his posture. A look of resignation replaced his blank expression.

"Who is Sarah Dumont?" I decided to start with the most painful possibility. "Is she your secret lover, too?"

Simmy leaned on his elbows, folded his hands into prayer position, and brought them to his nose. Then he shook his head.

I sighed with relief on the inside. "Is she your daughter?"

He paused for a moment, then slowly shook his head again.

"Is she a niece or something? Because she sure as heck isn't a stranger, Simmy. You clearly knew her for some time before all this happened."

Simmy stared at his beer as though he were carefully choosing his words. Then he unfolded his hands, placed them on the table, and looked me in the eye.

"I didn't know her for some time before this happened," he said.

More bullshit. I couldn't believe it. "That's a lie, Simmy. How can that possibly—"

"I've known her far longer than that. I've known her for most of her life." Simmy stopped talking. He looked around to make sure no one was listening.

My heartbeat thumped in my ear.

"I've known her for most of her life because she's the daughter of a friend of mine. And ironically enough, the favor I need you to do for me concerns this friend."

He motioned for me to lean forward. I did so, and then he did the same. I thought his breath would warm my ear but cabin airflow came on and a cold breeze gave me a shiver instead.

"Sarah Dumont's father is the President of Russia. She is the illegitimate daughter of my good friend and mentor, Valery Putler."

CHAPTER 27

The dead girl's lover was the daughter of the President of Russia. This was the same man who'd perpetuated the persecution of the gay community since taking office. For a moment, I couldn't shake the irony of the situation, even as the questions came tumbling to my mind, one after another. When I finally recouped my senses enough to speak, I kept my voice at a whisper, to make sure none of the crew or the bodyguards in the adjacent cabin area could hear me.

"Does Sarah Dumont know who her father is?" I said.

"Of course," Simmy said.

"That explains the arrogance."

"Arrogance?"

"Aloofness, arrogance, whatever you want to call it. She's weird, Simmy. Surely you can see that. That comment that no man would dare to kill her, when her father's identity is a secret. Who says things like that?"

Simmy shrugged.

"And she was strangely homophobic even though she was in a lesbian affair. She said something about having gay friends but not condoning the morality of their relationships. Does her father support her financially?"

"She's his daughter."

I pictured her property, the luxury cars, and her restaurant in Bruges.

"Her wanting to keep the police out of it makes sense now," I said. "The desire for privacy and all that. So does her lifestyle. I appreciate she's a successful artist, but she seemed to have more disposable income than I would have imagined."

"Sarah is set for life, as long as she remains discreet and respects her father."

"When you say discreet," I said, "you mean doesn't let anyone find out who her father is, or that she's had at least one lesbian relationship."

"In Russia, a man is expected to be a man. His reputation is very important, with his family, in business, and especially in politics. In Russia, having an illegitimate child would hurt an elected official's popularity."

I couldn't suppress a laugh, nor did I want to. "Elected?"

"Having a lesbian daughter would be even more unpopular. So as the saying goes, some things are better left unsaid."

I considered what I'd learned. "I guess I have to give Putler some credit, hard as that is to believe."

"Really? Why?"

"At least he acknowledges she's his daughter. At least he supports her, and I guess based on what you say, loves her to the best of his personal boundaries. That's a lot more than George Romanov can say."

"Valery Putler is not one-dimensional. He is not evil incarnate and he is not a monster. The Western press likes to make him out to be without redeeming qualities because every story needs a villain and he's a convenient one. But the truth is far more complicated. Do you know why he was tapped as to be president in the first place?"

I shook my head.

"Because he couldn't be bribed. He was the only KGB officer, which is to say the only Chekhist that his predecessor had ever met who had a reputation for integrity, who refused to take a pay-off."

"If that's true, then his former reputation makes him all the more disappointing since he took office," I said.

"He's been a positive influence on Sarah. He is, as you know, a Tae Kwon Do expert. He encouraged her to learn discipline and self-reliance through martial arts."

"Yeah, that didn't look like the first time she'd swept a guy's legs out from under him."

I remembered following Sarah Dumont to her gym where I saw heavy bags and men in training. I must have caught her on a day without martial arts practice. Had I followed her another day, I might have seen her sparring with those same men.

"It turns out the blossom didn't fall too far from the prover-bial tree," Simmy said. "She doesn't look like him. Physically, she clearly takes after her mother. But she's his spitting image in spirit."

"Meaning what, she wants to annex Ukraine, too?"

Simmy rolled his eyes. "If Valery wanted to annex Ukraine, the tanks would have rolled by now and no one would have stopped him. The only sound you would have heard from Europe and the States would have been the huffing and puffing of your gutless politicians. No, I mean Sarah is just like him in personality. She casts a giant shadow, she never retreats, and she never, ever surrenders."

"What about the home invasion in Amsterdam? Obviously whoever did it had no clue who she was, but whatever happened to the criminals? Did the police catch them, or did they ... disappear?"

"It never happened."

"What?"

"It was just a story she made up."

"Why make up something like that?" I said.

"To justify the security guards – whom her father insists on, by the way. And to get some privacy. Her father may support her but Sarah is legitimately successful in her own right. People in town know who she is, partly based on her success in dance, partly based on her lifestyle, the home, the cars, the girl about town. If you tell people you were the victim of a home invasion, they might not think twice if you're a recluse or a little bit odd."

"What about your relationship with her? If her identity is such a secret, how is it you've known her almost her entire life?"

Simmy's eyes danced all over the place, from me to his beer glass and to the widescreen television resting on a black lacquer bureau along one side of the plane. After giving me sufficient time to answer the question myself, they settled squarely on me again.

"Oh, my," I said. "You really are the son the President never had."

"First time I met her was right here in Amsterdam. She was seven years old. I was twenty-seven or twenty-eight, and Valery asked me to deliver a gift to a friend and her daughter. He gave me a sealed envelope, a big and thick one, like an accordion file, and told me to give it to the mother. When I asked him who the mother and girl were he told me he would take it as a personal favor if I would treat them as though they were my family."

"And you knew from that moment who they really were?"

"I didn't know, but I suspected. I did some due diligence of my own. You know, just out of curiosity. Sarah's mother was a Belgian born woman by the name of Stephanie Dumont. She was a dancer. When Valery was stationed in Berlin as a KGB agent in late nineteen eighties, she was performing in a revue at the Frie-drichstadt Palace. He was married at the time, but I think he fell in love, for real."

"Where is her mother now?"

"Portofino, Italy."

"And the man she refers to as her father? The one who made all the money in construction?"

"Doesn't exist. The mother, Stephanie Dumont, never married. It turned out she can fall in love with a man or a woman, but her preference is the latter. That's why she was in Berlin in the first place. It was the world's most friendly place for those kinds of people back then."

"Those kinds of people?"

"You know what I mean." Simmy blushed. "The gay people."

"Did you ever find out what was in that file you gave Sarah and her mother?"

"I assume it had some form of currency in it. Cash, bearer bonds, something like that. This was in 1999. He'd just taken office for the first time and he didn't know the banking system the way he does now."

"Spoken like the prodigal son," I said.

"Okay, he didn't control the banking system the way he does now."

"Spoken like a man searching for the truth."

"I'm trying. I met Sarah and her mother half a dozen more times during the next three or four years. They had my number if they needed anything. And then a few years later, Valery told me he would no longer need my help in this matter."

"Did he ever confirm Sarah was his daughter?"

"He did," Simmy said.

"When?"

"Last night."

"Last night?" I remembered Simmy pacing, mobile phone pressed to his ear, looking increasingly more relaxed as the hours passed. "You talked to Putler last night? While we were at the police station?"

"Of course I talked to him. His daughter was attacked. He deserved to know immediately."

I waited for Simmy to follow-up with the obvious, an admission of his personal reason for calling his mentor, who he feared had grown suspicious of his protégé's political aspirations. But no such confession followed. So I decided to keep staring at him until it did.

"What can I say," Simmy said. "You did me an enormous favor. You probably saved my business, and maybe even kept me out of jail."

"He's pleased?"

Simmy appeared incredulous. "Pleased? The man is overjoyed. I saved …" He cleared his throat. "We saved his daughter's life. No matter what else he is or is not, there is no doubt that Valery is a devoted father."

I remembered what George Romanov had told me, that Simmy had an ulterior motive for wanting to solve Iskra's murder and bring her killer to justice.

"Simmy," I said, and waited for him to give me his undivided attention.

He blinked casually and then froze. He knew me by now. He could tell by my curt tone and the intensity of my expression that I was perturbed by something, and that this something concerned him.

"What is it, love?"

He meant it in the British sense, I was sure. He lived in London and friends called each other "love" all the time, didn't they? Still, his choice of words distracted me.

What was my problem again? Oh, yes. That.

"Did you know Iskra's lover was Putler's daughter from the beginning? Is this why you hired me to find Iskra's killer in the first place?"

"Absolutely not." He answered firmly, emphatically, and without hesitation. "Iskra's mother is an old friend of mine, just like I said. We went to university together. Yes, we were more than friends for a few semesters but that was a long, long time ago. I was just as surprised that Sarah Dumont turned out to be the secret lover as you are to learn her father's identity."

"But once you got the license plate of that blue Porsche Macan," I said, "you knew."

"Yes. Then, I knew."

"But you didn't tell me."

"Tell you what?" Simmy said.

"Who she was. Who her father was."

"That would have been imprudent."

"Meaning you were afraid that her father being the Russian President might affect my performance. That I might be a bit less enthusiastic."

"You're putting words in my mouth."

"You didn't trust my professionalism or my ethics. A person isn't responsible for her father's actions."

Simmy glared at me. "Are we done?"

I pressed my lips together and returned his stare.

Simmy ate some duck, took a sip of beer and cleared his throat. "Sarah Dumont's father's true identity had no bearing on who killed Iskra Romanova. None whatsoever. Surely we can agree on that."

"I needed to tread lightly around her for my own personal safety, given all her security and her father's history of – how shall we put it – disposing of those who displease him?"

"Nonsense. I trusted your professionalism and your ethics completely."

I played with the shrimp on my plate. "You're my client. You don't owe me anything other than clarity and fair pay. But it would have been nice if you'd trusted me just a little bit more."

Simmy considered my comment for a moment and then gave me a quick, barely perceptible nod. "Agreed. I'm trying to be a better man. I'll do better next time."

"Next time?" I said, peppering my voice with some moxie. "You mean you're going to hire me again?"

"You're soon going to discover that I've been withholding even more information from you."

The mischief in his eyes suggested he was playing with me. And then I remembered the Russian nesting dolls and the key that I'd found. Amidst the attack on Sarah Dumont, Romanov's death and our quick departure, I hadn't dwelled on it. I'd pushed it aside as a pleasant mystery to contemplate once we reached London and my life normalized a bit.

"The *matryoshka*," I said. "I don't think I've fully grasped all its knowledge yet."

Simmy shrugged. "Obviously."

"Why is that so obvious?"

"Because if you'd solved its mystery and absorbed all its knowledge, I would know with a simple glance at your face."

"Really," I said. "That's a bold statement. Here's how I see the situation. My sense is that by giving me the *matryoshka*, you've given me a key, metaphorically speaking, and it's up to me to figure out what it opens. Does that sound right?"

I spied a twinkle in Simmy's eyes. "Well, that's an interesting way to put it. Perhaps you'll make some headway in London."

"Speaking of our arrival in London. You said you need a favor …"

"Sarah Dumont's father is overjoyed that his daughter survived this attempt on her life," Simmy said, "an attempt to kill her in the most brutal and inhumane way. He would like to thank the person who saved her personally."

"Huh?"

"Russian President Valery Putler ... he'd like to thank you in person. He'd like to shake your hand."

My blood pressure rose for reasons that weren't entirely clear to me. Sure, I considered the man to be a mass murderer and an evil despot, but that didn't mean I couldn't do a favor for a client and shake the man's hand. Did it?

"Okay," I said. "No problem. You seem to think this is a big deal. Is there something you know that I don't know?"

Simmy narrowed his eyes. "This is an important moment for me, Nadia. I did good for him. He's most grateful. It's an opportunity for me to give him a hug, remind him of my loyalty to him. It's a chance to shift any paranoia he may have about someone trying to usurp his power away from me."

"I get that," I said. "What does that have to do with my meeting him so he can thank me?"

"I can't have you getting into it with him."

My jaw literally fell open. Fortunately, I wasn't chewing any food at the time. "Excuse me?"

"You're the strong Ukrainian woman——"

"Ukrainian-American woman."

"Who's proud of her ancestral heritage."

"And this is a problem because?"

"Valery can be provocative. Sometimes he says things that can be shocking to a foreigner not used to his manner or his sense of humor. I can see him saying something that offends your feminist or ethnic or some other Nadia sensibility ..."

I feigned shock and mouthed the word. "Me?"

"And I simply can't have that," Simmy said. "I need this to be a friendly meet and greet, filled with love, joy and fine manners all around."

I recalled George Romanov describing me as the American whore with Russian bloodlines. I had little doubt I was going to shake the hand of a man who would think of me in the same light, or worse. *But what did I care what he thought of me?*

"Have you given thought to how you'll describe me to him?" I said.

Simmy frowned. "What are talking about?"

"How you'll introduce me to the President of Russia. Will you say I'm your friend——"

"God no. Russian men don't have female friends."

"Your investigator?" I said.

"Better."

"Or your dietary whip mistress?"

"Oh, he'd have a party with that one," Simmy said.

"And if I shake his hand and act like a European lady, that will help keep you in his good graces?"

"God willing."

"Then it's settled," I said.

We turned our attention back to our dinners. The attendants checked on us again. After they left I asked my one remaining question. I'd purposefully waited until our conversation seemed to have ended on a congenial note in hopes that Simmy would drop his guard and I'd be able to measure his body language when he heard my query.

"Is there any truth to it?" I said.

Simmy looked up from his plate, food in mouth, genuinely confused.

"Did you ever whisper, even in the quietest tones, to the most trusted of friends, under the influence of adult beverages or not, that you could do a better job as President of Russia, even in jest?"

Simmy glanced at me with a stoic expression and then averted my eyes, leaving me with the distinct impression that he'd made at least one such proclamation.

"Since you asked a personal question ..." he said.

"You have one for me?"

Simmy studied me. "I believe you're a passionate person who loves life, but sometimes I get the sense that you're incapable of trusting another human being, especially a man. And there is a melancholy about you. I see it in your eyes and hear it in your voice, and it leaves me wondering, what is it that caused you to become an isolationist?"

I laughed, out of self-defense as much as confusion over his choice of words. "A what?"

"An isolationist. You are like the country that doesn't want anything to do with any other country. You might conduct some trade, but you don't want to be intimate. You look only inward. You never speak of men. You never speak of boyfriends. Why do you insist on being alone?"

Deflections, excuses and lies flooded my mind. Anything but the truth, for I couldn't stomach thinking about it let alone the humiliation of revealing it to anyone else. And yet I found myself reaching for words that at least broached the subject. A need propelled me, the same kind I'd heard in Simmy's voice when he'd begged me to come here.

"My first husband cheated on me," I said.

Simmy waited a beat. "I'm very sorry."

"We were living in New York. He commuted to his job in New Haven. One day he was giving a lecture in Hartford at Trinity College. My mother called me in an agitated state. She said her date was drunk and determined to take advantage of her. She refused to call the police because the guy was a fellow immigrant she'd known a long time. So I called my husband and told him to drive out to her house. The roads were slick from hail and he had this old Volkswagen with bald tires, and when he said it was too dangerous I told him to get his dick out of his little red-head's mouth and go save his mother-in-law."

I stopped because I knew Simmy could figure out the rest for himself.

"I remember you told me your husband died in a car crash. That was the night."

"That was the night."

Simmy took a moment to think about it. I considered speaking some more but I simply couldn't go there.

"It wasn't your fault," Simmy said. "You blame yourself for his death, you think you're unworthy of another man. You are too intelligent for that, Nadia. You must stop that kind of thinking at once.

"Yeah," I said.

Ever the oligarch issuing orders about what I should and should not think, but I still loved him for asking. No one else gave a shit, and he was right. I didn't let them. In truth, I didn't feel guilty about my husband's death at all. It was his choice to drive fifty miles per hour around the bend to complete his errand and get back to his lover as quickly as possible.

"We are alike then," Simmy said. "We are both damaged goods."

"Oh, yeah," I said.

"Shall we make a fresh start when we land?"

"You bet."

I might have gone on to finish my dinner in a genuinely pleasant state of mind if I'd told him the complete truth.

But I hadn't.

CHAPTER 28

We landed at terminal five at Heathrow. A limousine picked us up and drove us a few hundred yards to an unmarked white door. It looked like an entrance for airport personnel or the door to a storage room for equipment, but in fact it was the portal to the Windsor Room, Heathrow's VIP lounge.

Inside, bonsai trees flanked white leather sofas and chairs beneath a bombproof glass roof. A man resembling the Dali Lama stood talking to a man resembling the actor, Tom Hardy, in one corner. A party from the Middle East, men dressed in dark business suits and white robes alike, occupied another.

Russian President Valery Putler's entourage took up center stage. Six bodyguards surrounded his sofa. All of them stood at attention with their hands by their sides and their eyes on the interior of the suite.

As soon as he saw Simmy, Putler burst out smiling. He rose to his feet, ignored his bodyguards, and headed our way. He bounded more than he walked, with a strange hitch in his step. He looked like the kid in school who was determined to compensate for his diminutive stature by walking like a tough guy. He was compact, svelte and fit in a perfectly tailored suit but a bit puffy in the face, as though he'd attended one too many Botox parties.

He embraced Simmy, kissed him on both cheeks and appeared to have tears in his eyes when he grasped Simmy by the shoulders.

"Thank you, my friend. Thank you so much."

Simmy bowed his head. His face flushed and he seemed to be trying hard not to smile like a child who'd pleased an impossible parent. Then he quickly gathered himself and introduced me.

"Mr. President, this is Nadia Tesla. This is the woman who is truly responsible for both our happiness. She's the one who deserves your thanks."

"Thank you, Miss Nadia Tesla," Putler said, "for your service on behalf of this girl, who is very special to me. I am deeply indebted to you."

"You're welcome," I said.

Putler beamed and looked me over. At first I was flattered — he seemed so genuinely grateful. I forgot his reputation and his misdeeds, real and alleged. He was a world leader and he was thanking me. How could I not be gracious? But then his expression seemed to morph from smile to grin, or perhaps that's what it had been all along and I was just too naïve to realize it. There was a lasciviousness to the curl of his lips that gave me a creepy vibe that I'd just been measured, evaluated and appraised on the basest physical level.

"Since you're an American," Putler said, turning serious, "I want to tell you something. Yes, I love cranes and tigers. And polar bears and snow leopards. Oh, how I love the snow leopard. But I love blue jays and butterflies, too. These lies that your American magazine spread about me ... That I'm some kind of asswipe that takes pictures of the great carnivores to show that I'm in command of them ... that is complete and total crap."

I was so stunned by his choice of words and his obsession about what some periodical had written about him that I didn't know what to say. So I just nodded, like a sympathetic asswipe.

"If I wanted to be that guy ... If I wanted to show the world that I can tame the beast, I'd take pictures of the T-Rex I've had genetically re-created at my compound from a pre-historic DNA sample." He leaned toward me, eyes afire. "Jurassic Park," he said in broken English, before switching back to Russian. "It is fiction no more. It is a reality and it is mine." He pulled his neck back. "How would you like to show the world some pictures of that?"

I had to take a moment to make sure he was joking, which his wink and grin finally confirmed.

"At first I wasn't sure if you were kidding," I said. "You spoke with so much ... conviction."

"As opposed to?" Putler said.

"An American politician."

Putler let out a belly laugh and pointed at Simmy. "I see why this one likes you to order dinner for him. He told me you have Russian bloodlines, so it doesn't surprise me that we get along well, you know?"

"Not Russian," I said without thinking. "Ukrainian."

"Excuse me?"

"My parents. And their parents. They were Ukrainian. Not Russian."

Only after I'd corrected Putler did I notice the cloud that had descended over Simmy's face.

Oops.

Putler smiled and shrugged. "It's the same thing, sweetheart. There's no such country as Ukraine. Ukrainians are proper Russians. Always have been. Always will be."

"Then why are you bombing them?"

A hint of irritation crossed Putler's face, but it was quickly replaced with the thoughtful look of an experienced statesman. "I'm not bombing them. Someone has misinformed you. It's my duty to protect and support all Russian people no matter where they live. If my support results in Ukraine re-joining the Russian empire, so be it. You see, you're American, and you don't understand something very basic."

"What's that?" I said.

"Ukraine has no leadership because they're basically Russian peasants. They need to be led by a Russian. Your Western press lies to you and tells you I'm bombing them. No, that is not true. What I'm doing is saving them. Putler leaned into my ear. "We'll leave the bombing for the Poles. No one ever had any use for them." He pulled his head back and winked. Then a lunatic's smile spread on his face. "And after them, who knows?" He switched to broken English and sang softly. "Oh say, can you see, by the dawn's early light ..." He stopped singing and winked again.

He sounded unhinged, which was ironic because I felt as though I were coming unhinged, as though I knew I should play dumb and walk away but I simply couldn't deny my urge to set his ass straight. Blaspheming motherfucker, I thought. And then I caught Simmy smiling out of the corner of my eye. It was a forced smile by a desperate man because I could see him begging me with his eyes ...

I reached out and brushed Putler's arm with my fingers. "Just let me know ahead of time, Mr. President," I said. "so I can escape to my ancestral homeland in time. Just me and my kitty. She looks just like a snow leopard, you know."

Putler grinned as though that bonded us for life. He proceeded to remove a business card from his wallet. Then he raised his hand over his shoulder, snapped his fingers, and made a writing motion with the same hand. In a flash, a bodyguard was slipping a pen into his hand.

"A Russian man always pays his debts," Putler said, as he scribbled something on the card. "As a token of thanks. I'd like to offer you a gift." He finished writing and handed me the card.

I took it.

"I've granted you a favor."

"A favor?"

"Yes. One favor. My private number is on that card. If there is ever anything I can do to help you, you can reach out to me. And if I can help you, I will."

I stared at the card. It fascinated, repulsed and electrified me. This had to be one of world's ultimate get-out-of-jail free cards, and regardless of the morals of the man who'd underwritten the guarantee, it was mine.

"Now, if you'll excuse us," Putler said, "I have to talk to this guy in private for a minute. Maybe he can give me some advice on how to make some money."

Putler punched Simmy playfully in the shoulder. Simmy cast a look of gratitude at me as he followed Putler to his leather sofa.

I waited off to the side, pleased with myself. I could have gone off on Putler. In my younger, less prudent days, I probably would have done just that. But now I had clients to please and a man to impress. I hated to admit that, but whom was I fooling? And based on the look Simmy had given me before he'd walked away with his mentor, I'd succeeded.

Less than five minutes later, Simmy returned, slipped his hand along the curve of my back and guided me toward the white door.

"How did it go?" I said, as soon as we were outside.

"Fantastic," Simmy said.

"Is he always that way?"

"What way?"

"Insane," I said.

Simmy chuckled. "I told you he can sound eccentric to people who don't know him well. Maybe he was even a bit odder today, but who can blame him? The man's been under a lot of pressure himself. In fact, the man's under constant pressure."

"But the two of you?" I said. "You're good?"

Simmy allowed himself a grin, which was the equivalent of a full-fledged smile for most men. "He is so grateful. I reaffirmed my loyalty to him and he told me he wants us both to join him for Christmas Eve this year."

"Both of us?"

Simmy patted my lower back. "I have to stop by my head-quarters in London and take a meeting with some financiers. I'll have my driver take you to the Grosvenor. You can check in, refresh yourself, and then I'll meet you for lunch. We start with a drink at the hotel bar, yes?"

"Yes," I said.

"Good. In the meantime, when you get to your hotel room, be certain to secure your valuables in the hotel safe. London is a crazy town. You can never be too cautious."

It was finally over. The murder had, indeed, been part of a more complex maze of problems that Simmy needed help resolving. And I'd helped him resolve them.

All that was left was for me to collect my reward.

CHAPTER 29

After checking into the hotel, I took a long shower and changed into sweatpants and a t-shirt. I was about to lie down on the bed and check my e-mails when I remembered Simmy's advice about using the safe. I always secured my valuables when I left the room, but I never worried about them when I was in the hotel, especially not with my door bolted shut from the inside. I saw no reason to do so this time, either, but decided to take a look at it and set the code for later use.

I found the safe in a bureau near the mini-bar. To my dismay, a cardboard sign rested beside the safe. The note read "Out of Order" and had additional writing below it, but the print was so small I had to lift the sign and bring it closer to my eyes to read it. It said, "Please call the front desk to secure your valuable items."

I reached out to put the sign back in its place. A circle of shiny steel caught my eye. It was the slot for a master key to the safe, one that provided emergency access in case a guest secured a valuable and the locking mechanism failed.

Simmy had insisted I use the safe. I hadn't thought much of it at the time, especially given how he'd phrased the suggestion, reminding me that London could be a dangerous city.

Now his words sounded off.

I tossed the sign onto the bed and hurried to my bag, fumbled with my purse and pulled out the key I'd found hidden inside the Russian nesting doll.

Then I skipped back to the safe, placed the tip of the key into the hole and pushed. The key slid into its grooves, accompanied by a glorious metallic zipping noise. I turned the key in a clockwise fashion.

The door popped open.

A green velvet box beckoned.

I pulled it out and opened it.

A diamond ring shimmered inside. It was an Asscher cut, larger than your average marble and slightly smaller than the planet Mars. It scintillated like fire and ice.

My first thought was nil. I stood paralyzed by a completely alien sensation. My second thought was that there'd been some sort of mistake. This ring could not possibly be for me. My third thought was the recognition of the alien sensation for what it was, unfettered and boundless joy.

I ran to the bed, jewelry box in hand, grabbed my phone, and dialed his number.

"Did you find it?" he said.

I sniffed in the tears. "You're a bigger fool than I am."

"I want all of you. I want the intelligence, the will, and the passion. I want the irreverence, the scars, and all your insecurities. I want to be the father of your children. You are the bravest, smartest, sexiest woman in the world."

I had to breathe deeply before I could answer in a manner that befit my whip mistress reputation. "And you are a man of impeccable taste."

"You really think I have good taste?"

I glanced at my ring. It shimmered and sparkled, gaudy yet classy, outrageous yet desirable at the same time. Just like the man who'd given it to me.

"It has potential," I said. "Add the right woman's touch ..."

"Speaking of your touch," he said.

"Yes?"

"The meeting went faster than I expected."

My joy was momentary. The dark cloud that hung over my existence reappeared and reminded me that I was still persecuted by my prior marriage.

"There's something you need to know, Simmy," I said. "Something about my past."

"Whatever it is you have to tell me," Simmy said, "if it's about your past, then it's in the past. It's not going to change anything."

"I don't want it to ruin this day."

"Then tell me now and set yourself free."

I took a deep breath, and the memories came flooding back.

"My husband's lover – the graduate student – came to his funeral," I said. "She was breathtaking. If a cherry blossom were to turn into a woman, it would look like her. I wasn't surprised he'd fallen for her. I never thought I quite measured up to his standards. When I walked up to her and told her I knew who she was and how dare she show her face, she expressed her condolences, for my husband's death, and for how he'd deceived me. She did it very sweetly, with tears in her eyes, as though she was my little sister."

"I don't understand," Simmy said.

I had to take a deep breath to continue, and much as I tried to fortify my voice, it crackled. "It turned out she wasn't my husband's lover. He wasn't having an affair with her. He was having an affair with his male graduate assistant. He was gay all along. I was so fixated on having a Ukrainian-American husband, on pleasing my mother, on perpetuating Ukrainian-American culture the way my father had wanted, I lived in denial the whole time. I wasn't his wife. I was just his beard."

Simmy asked me to explain what I meant by that word. I told him.

"Your ex-husband was a coward," Simmy said. "Unlike Iskra Romanova and Sarah Dumont, he didn't have the courage to be his own man. I am very proud of you for sharing this with me, and I'm going to tell you something about myself and make you a promise."

"What's that?"

"I'm not fond of facial hair. So you can rest assured that I will never grow a beard, and my wife will never be one."

I sniffed in some more tears and laughed.

"I like it when you laugh," he said, "but tell me. Why are you still talking to me? I'm going to beat you to the bar. You're going to be late for the beginning of the rest of your life ..."

"Ha! We'll see about that. "Come to me," I said.

"I'm on my way, love."

CHAPTER 30

I ended the call, wiped the tears from my eyes, and changed into a sleek but understated blue cocktail dress that hugged my body. Then I flew downstairs, determined to beat Simmy to the bar so that I could see him enter. So that I could watch all eyes turn his way while I sat there thinking *"that's my man."*

The tavern was dark, elegant and glorious, with paneled walls and gilded fixtures at the bar. Cliques of well-dressed folks drank in groups at small tables appointed with upholstered furnishings that were scattered around the room. Two grizzled bartenders tended to a bar area that buzzed with lunch activity. A television hung from a wall behind the bar.

My hunger for some tasty food was exceeded only by my thirst. I wanted a tall drink, the kind with no bottom. I walked to the far side of the room to an empty stool and took a seat, eyes glued to the entrance on the lookout for Simmy. After the bartender took my order for a glass of ice water, I glanced at the television monitor over the bar. Just as the image of Valery Putler appeared, I caught sight of Simmy entering the bar.

One of his bodyguards was in front of him, the other behind him. Simmy's eyes found mine. They looked at me adoringly and he gave me the slightest nod. I fought the urge to slice my way though the bodies and jump into his arms. Instead, the television monitor seemed to draw me in as though it had a power of its own.

Putler was standing at a lectern next to the prime minister of Germany, surrounded by men in suits and overcoats. His lips were moving and he was gesturing with his hands.

"Putler Arrives in Berlin for Economic Summit," the caption read. And in the bottom of the right corner of the screen, an additional word in italics informed the viewing public: "LIVE."

I glanced back to Simmy. While his bodyguard cleared the way for him, a random customer beside me addressed one of the bartenders with a booming request for a black and tan. His mellifluous baritone drew my attention. When I looked over, an unremarkable bald man rose from his seat beside the man with the baritone.

The balding man left the bar and brushed by Simmy.

A mist formed in the air.

Simmy froze. His entire face seemed to seize up.

Our eyes met.

I saw only horror.

He fell to the ground.

The bodyguards fell with him.

I remembered what Simmy had told me, that when bodyguards fall it means the man they're guarding has been assassinated, and that they too, have been poisoned.

My heart urged me to rush forward, but my survival skills prevailed. I counted three more suits on the floor. Instead of moving forward toward the man whose ring I was wearing, I retreated. My feet felt like cinderblocks, the floor like quicksand. But what I was learning now was that sometimes your only salvation is to keep your eyes open and your mouth shut, place one foot backward, drag the other one to it, and repeat.

In the background, a man continued delivering an impassioned speech on the television.

He was the man who'd expressed his gratitude in person for saving his daughter's life by giving me a business card that granted me one special favor.

If only I had used it. It had never occurred to me that by granting me one favor, Putler had given me a chance to save Simmy's life.

I escaped the bar, stepped outside the hotel, and dialed the number Putler had given me. No one picked up for obvious reasons. So I walked around the hotel and kept dialing continuously. Sirens sounded and brakes screeched in the background. I don't know how many loops I made or how much time passed, but eventually someone finally picked up my call. I froze in place on the sidewalk, but there was no sound on the other end of the line. An awkward pause followed, and I feared I was so distraught that I'd been misdialing the entire time.

And then I heard his voice on the other end of the line.

"If you're calling me to ask for the resurrection of your fiancé," Putler said, "I haven't acquired that skill yet. But my scientists are working on it. They tell me they're getting close."

"What a fool believes," I said.

He paused and sighed with great delight. "I couldn't have said it better myself."

I took a breath to compose myself. "You do still owe me a favor, though, don't you?"

"I'm a man of my word. Just understand that drinking from the cooling pond in Chernobyl and that sort of thing doesn't qualify. It has to be a reasonable request."

I couldn't believe he'd mentioned Chornobyl. It simply couldn't be a coincidence. Somehow, Valery Putler – *the President of Russia* – knew that I'd snuck in there illegally two years ago.

"It's agreed then," I said. "We'll speak again."

"I look forward to it, my snow leopard."

He ended the call.

I thought of the *matryoshka*.

It contained seven dolls. Simmy had told me that I needed to know all seven dolls to understand a Russian man.

Now I understood the one who'd outsmarted me.

He was a powerful statesman, an avid sportsman, and a devoted father. He was also an insecure boy, a thug, a liar, and a murderer.

He was whichever of these men he needed to be to meet his objective.

He was all the other men, too.

ABOUT THE AUTHOR

Orest Stelmach is a mystery and thriller writer and the author of the Nadia Tesla series. His novels have been Kindle #1 bestsellers, optioned for film development, and translated into numerous foreign languages. Prior to becoming a full-time writer, Orest was an institutional investment portfolio manager for over twenty years. He is a graduate of Dartmouth College and the University of Chicago Booth School of Business.

Made in the USA
Coppell, TX
03 September 2020

35631006R00146